AF485016

Martha —
The Vineyard Legend

Maxwell Burnham

Martha — The Vineyard Legend

This is a work of fiction. Names, characters, places, and incidents are either the product of the author's imagination or are used fictitiously. Any resemblance to actual events, locales, or persons, living or dead, is entirely coincidental.

First Edition, 2026

Published by Red Cliff Press

United States of America

ISBN: 979-8-9931578-0-1

—*Dedication*—

To the people of Noepe — the original "land between waters", past, present, and future. To the Wampanoag, whose presence, language, and courage remain the heartbeat of the island. To the eternal island spirit that shaped this legend, and to those who encouraged me to listen

A Note to Readers

In this story you'll see words from **Wôpanâak**, the language of the **Wampanoag** people.

They're first seen in **bold** so you can spot them easily. Some mean simple things — like **wetu** (house) or **namohs** (fish). Others are names or chants that carry deeper meaning.

At the back of the book you'll find a Glossary with pronunciations and translations. But don't worry — you don't have to stop and check every time. Like Martha, you'll soon pick them up as you go.

Learning a few Wampanoag words is part of the adventure — a way of hearing the island's original voice.

WuneeKeesoq, netomp

(Good spirit, friend)

— Nokamoset

England – Autumn 1599

Elizabeth awoke with a jolt. Something was rustling in the hay nearby. Shards of morning light cut through gaps in the barn roof above. Two men were shouting at each other outside. One voice rose above the other, laced with venom, orders and threats. Panicked and desperate, Elizabeth realized she must have slept past her chance to escape. She looked around for a possible way out. Nothing. She pressed deeper into the hay. The stench of mold and cow dung burned at her throat. The straw scratched her arms and legs.

"Elizabeth Montgomery!" Her name sounded like a curse through one man's clenched teeth. "A striking beauty of fifteen years, perhaps. Looks to be older. Chestnut hair. Bright blue eyes. She wore a dress of green satin yesterday, but I wager she'll be in rags by now, the spoiled wench. She carries stolen treasures too — jewelry and coins enough to bribe fools like you. Have you seen her?"

Elizabeth froze. Lord Goodwin Morgrave. She recognized his voice from her father's study. He was the ambitious young barrister sworn to enforce her marriage to some old crony by her father's order. A man whose death would double her father's fortune — only if she bore his offspring. Elizabeth would rather die first.

Her chest clenched as the farmer muttered something she could barely hear. Then Morgrave's voice sharpened, each word edged with iron.

"Harboring a fugitive will see you ruined! Do you understand, dullard? This girl belongs to me. I will scour every cursed barn and byre in this county until she is dragged to heel!"

The farmer stammered, swearing on his mother's life that no girl had set foot on the farm but his own daughter. "I – I have no secrets. Search wherever you wish, sir. You will find nothing but the worthless clutter of a poor tenant farmer."

Elizabeth backed deeper into the straw. She stifled a scream when she felt the sharp claws of a rat as it scurried across her hand. Her eyes burned from the dust and grime.

The barn door complained with a squeal when Morgrave threw it open. Elizabeth's breath stopped. The old floor shuddered with each step he took, "Miss Montgomery? — Your father misses you — Lizzie-Beth? I mean you no harm, dear?"

His shadow fell across the barn floor as he seized a pitchfork and drove it savagely into the mound of hay. The tines ripped inches from her ribs. She bit down on a cry, the iron taste of blood on her tongue. She dared not move an inch; straw cascading over her face. Again, the fork plunged, a foot from her shoulder. Again, a breath from her leg.

At last he snarled, hurled the fork at the farmer with a curse, and stormed out. The petrified farmer lingered for a moment, looking around his barn quizzically. Then he chased after Morgrave pleading for mercy, knowing his life hung in the balance. Nothing good ever came from the notice of wealthy men. By the time he reached the lane, the ill-tempered barrister was already in his carriage, moving on to the next farm.

Elizabeth listened in silence before she sat up. Pigeons cooed from the rafters above. A cow bellowed in a nearby pasture. Hunting dogs were howling in the distance. She looked down, dismayed. Her beautiful dress was now a mess, covered in muck and detritus from the barn floor. She searched around for anything to change her appearance. A tattered blanket hung on a stall door. A few things hung on the wall nearby. Her hands shook as she seized the farmer's filthy work coat and britches from a peg. The stench made her gag. She quickly stripped off her torn dress and jammed it into a feed sack. She felt for the gold locket at her throat, cool against her skin, recalling the day her mother gave it to her. She stuffed dirt and straw into the coin purse at her waist to muzzle the clink of metal. In moments she was out the back, stumbling down a cow path, ragged clothes hanging loose, the sack slung over her shoulder.

The farmland gave way to the forest and overgrown fields. She kept to the shadows, darting from tree to tree. Once she glimpsed highwaymen in a rough camp ahead, their laughter loud and careless. She ducked through nettles, keeping low until they vanished. Her father's world of parlors and music rooms seemed a lifetime away; now mud streaked her legs, thorns tore at her sleeves and her hair clung in damp tangles.

By midday she had reached the coast. A sharp salty wind bit at her cheeks, making her eyes water. The uneven stone rubble made her stumble while mats of slimy seaweed threatened to toss her into the waves. Families ignored her struggle as they strolled along the strand, children laughing, fishermen hauling their catch — a beautiful sunny day for them. For her, every gull's cry was an alarm, every voice seemed a threat.

In time, she neared a village with a giant stone wharf and a few ships lashed alongside. After climbing up from the shore, she slipped among a group of women mending nets in the shadows. They paid her no mind as she crouched close, pretending to untangle a knot of rope. Their chatter hid her for a moment, but she felt exposed. Too many eyes to describe this fair skinned girl no one had seen before. She crept into a boathouse, the air thick with tar and salt. Her stomach growled. For the first time since the barn she let her shoulders sag, her body quivering with exhaustion.

"Girl!"

She spun around. A grizzled old fisherman filled the doorway, nets slung over his arm, eyes narrowing at the sight of her. "What are you doing in here?"

Elizabeth bolted past him before he could take a step after her.

❦

She burst into the chaos of the wharf — carts rumbling over cobbles, barrels rolling, gulls shrieking, sailors shouting. She pushed through fishmongers and porters, the stink of brine and guts filled her lungs. For one heartbeat she believed she was lost in the din, safe at last.

Then a sharp voice cut through it all.

Morgrave. Close by.

Her chest seized. Without thought she clambered into a wagon piled with barrels and crates. She pressed herself flat as the dock-hands heaved it up the gangplank of a nearby ship. She trembled in the shadows, whispering to herself: *He won't follow me here. He's searching for a girl, not a sailor.* Men around her shouted orders in Gaelic as the cart was eventually lowered deep into the cavernous hold. Elizabeth felt her tension release as the hatch above closed.

A new strategy formed in her mind, the sun would set soon and she could escape in the darkness. By then, Morgrave would be miles away, mercilessly torturing some new farmer or fisherman in his fruitless search for her. Elizabeth dared to believe she had slipped free. She pulled a bit of canvas over her head and gave a sigh of relief. The rhythm of lapping waves and creaking timbers eventually lulled her to sleep despite the gnawing fear that she still might be caught.

Elizabeth awoke in darkness to the pitch and roll of a ship at sea. She felt a raw twisting sickness in her stomach pulling the emptiness to her throat as her head throbbed in pain. Was it the few oats she had scavenged on the run? She felt around for the feed bag near the barrels and boxes with a sudden panic. It was gone! Did she drop it as she hid on the cart? Her dress! She patted the coin purse on her waist and felt for the locket at her neck, reassured they were still there.

Elizabeth peeked out from the canvas. The lower

deck was stacked to the rafters with barrels marked in various languages. Light filtered down through a few open hatches fore and aft of her hiding place. She listened as the deck above thundered with bustling crew. Gulls shrieked over a turbulent sea. The fright of an unknown destiny crawled into her thoughts. Stories of foreign lands and monstrous beasts made her heart race. The dream of his voice bellowed above them all. She put it out of her mind, and yet it seemed to echo back from above.

"Turn back immediately! By order of the King! I will not be carried off like this!" Morgrave shook the feed-bag with Elizabeth's dress streaming in the wind like a flag, "By God, I will have that minx —"

The captain's responded with a frustrated mix of Gaelic and English, absolute. "We are bound west, my lord. The tide takes us to the New World. You'll see no English shore till spring."

Elizabeth's blood froze.

Morgrave had been forced aboard — and now the ocean lashed them together, hunter and quarry joined by the same fate. His fury rang across the deck, a vow she knew in her bones would haunt her to her grave.

Noepe Island — Summer 1624

Off the southern coast of New England there lies an island the old ones call **Noepe** — the land between the streams. It rises from the sea like an echo of another world, shaped by winds, tides, and time.

The red clay cliffs of **Aquinnah** stand watch at the western edge, their layers worn like old stories. Pines lean eastward from the salt-kissed hills. Deer leave narrow paths in hidden meadows where the fox grapes cling to gnarled hedgerows. Osprey wheel overhead while harbor seals blink up from glistening coves. There is a rhythm on this island, deep and unspoken — older than the marks on ancient mariner's maps.

In time, foreign sailors called it a vineyard, for the vast tangle of wild grapes from slope to shore. But this name was not theirs to give. Her name was calling – carried on the wind, whispered by the sea, and written in the heart of a girl whose spirit dwells there for all time . . .

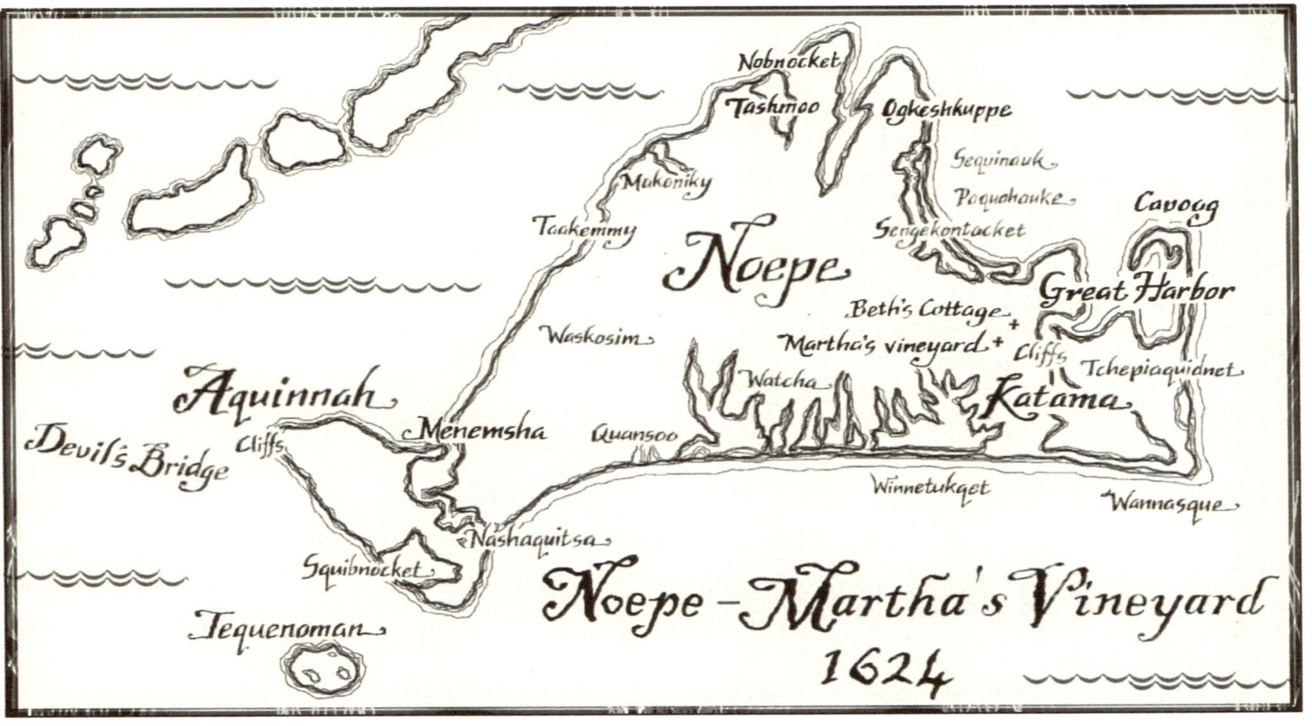

Nobnocket
Tashmoo
Ogkeshkuppe
Sequinauk
Poquahauke
Cavogg
Makoniky
Sengekontacket
Taakemmy
Noepe
Great Harbor
Beth's Cottage +
Martha's vineyard +
Cliffs
Tchepiaquidnet
Waskosim
Watcha
Katama
Aquinnah
Devil's Bridge
Cliffs
Menemsha
Quansoo
Winnetukget
Wannasque
Nashaquitsa
Squibnocket
Tequenoman
Noepe – Martha's Vineyard
1624

— *Chapter 1* —

Nestled in a hollow of old-growth forest where the oaks grew wide and deeply rooted, a worn little cottage seemed almost hidden from time itself. The path that led to it was narrow and overgrown, winding between sun-dappled stone walls and moss-thick trunks, until it opened with a hush into a clearing ringed by vines. Beth's small garden was surrounded by a tangle of wild fox grapes that crept along the edges of the grove like a living fence, their leaves flickering green and gold in the shifting light. The air held a softness there, filtered through high branches and the faint perfume of crushed fruit and damp wood. A wooden cart leaned against a cedar post. Sheep grazed together as their tails wagged contentedly. Blue-glass bottles caught light in the windows. And above it all, the roof sloped like an old shoulder, patched with driftwood and cedar shakes, as if the house itself had grown from the earth beneath it. Here, hidden from the village road and protected by the quiet murmurs of forest and vine, Auntie Beth, known as "Elizabeth" many years ago, kept her thoughts — and her secrets — hidden.

She sat on the wooden floor of the cottage, the dawn light slanting across the worn boards as she paused to dip a feather quill in a **popôq** shell inkwell. The diary lay open on a small box in her lap—its pages uneven, the leather cover softened by years and secrets. She wrote in careful script, the lines flowing with the elegance of a girl born into a life of refinement but aged by hardship. She missed her youth back home in England, not too many years ago, though an age of harrowing experiences.

As she reached the end of her latest entry, an uneasy chill crept up her spine. Was someone outside? She moved to hide the diary in its usual place—beneath the loose board under the hearth mat—but in her haste—fumbled. The book slipped and fell to the floor, open to a page near the beginning. She caught a glimpse of the entry recalled from her first storm-tossed voyage at sea. Disturbing visions of life aboard that cursed ship haunted her memories; the scratched lines of ink ghostly in the weak morning light. And she read:

"It was a fortnight of roaring black water, a shrieking wind like no voice I'd heard before. The sea clawed at the hull around me. Somewhere above, a man with hair the color of fire and cruel gray eyes as cold as ice had boarded the vessel just after me. For weeks I barely escaped from him, constantly running day and night. He didn't know I was aboard. I had to stay hidden or be dragged back to my family's estate."

She remembered the way she had crouched below deck for days, paying the ship's boy with the last coins from her purse in exchange for bread and silence. When the silver ran out, she had reluctantly parted with a bracelet—

the most precious thing that belonged to her mother. The boy took it greedily and left her begging for table scraps like a dog.

A soft knock at the cottage door startled her. She closed the diary, slipped it into the box, and tucked it away under the hearth mat. A moment later, **Pashanok**—her love, her **Wampanoag** warrior—gave the gentle call of a whippoorwill. A jolt of excitement surged through her as she opened the door. Broad-shouldered and lean from years on the water and in the hunt, his long black hair, loosely bound in a deerskin cord, fell across his back. A gold locket hung from his neck, her image inside—the only evidence of her lost beauty. His eyes, dark as wet clay, softened when they found her; the smallpox scars on her face were no barrier to his devotion.

"Where's my girl?" he asked, his voice soft but edged with a look of concern.

Beth hesitated. "Tending to her vineyard . . . or out wandering like she always does . . . "

His jaw tightened. "Did **Môs**i ask, or just go?"

She offered a wistful smile. Beth sometimes forgot she was only twelve — not yet grown, not yet hardened by the world. "Martha's strong like her father. And stubborn like her mother."

Without another word, he stepped back into the wind and left to search for his girl—Môsi, their beloved daughter Martha.

— *Chapter 2* —

The sun had just cleared the eastern rim of the island when Martha slipped through the meadow, silently savoring the early morning hour. Dew clung to the grass in cold pearls that soaked her bare feet. She loved the soft feeling between her toes on cool summer mornings. The path dipped into a hollow where the wind fell silent and the morning light turned gold and green, filtered through the trembling leaves.

Here, the wildness of the island gentled into a place she had made her own. A tumble of old stones, half-buried in moss, marked what might once have been a planting wall, laid long ago. She had cleared them enough to train her vines against the sheltering slope, weaving thin stakes and driftwood trellises to lift the curling tendrils into the sun. Grapes hung in loose green clusters, skins still hard— August-green, a month away from ripening. The air smelled of earth and leaves and the faint sweetness of blossoms somewhere beyond sight.

Martha had the wiry grace of a dancer or young deer. She was athletic in a way that made her a match for her Wampanoag cousin **Tobiasquash**, though she'd never say so. Her skin was a soft ruddy light brown, like the red cliffs of Aquinnah—with bright blue eyes and an inner vision that had grown clearer each season. Her black **wunnêgin** hair leaped about in wild curls, though she kept it pulled back with a bit of purple yarn, letting only a few rebellious strands bounce free; it would flash a bit of red in the bright sunlight. Freckles danced across her nose and cheeks, a point of teasing from her cousins, but she bore them with pride. She had a habit of tucking flowers into her hair, and of eating wild berries as she walked through her vineyard. The dress she wore most frequently was a favorite, though it had a curious history. It once belonged to a wealthy couple's only daughter who tragically died too young—a donation to the orphanage that Auntie Beth had reworked. Random stains were stitched over with embroidery by Martha herself: grapes, flowers, curling vines. Each design a living memory stitched into the cloth with her creative touch.

When Martha was nearly seven or eight years old, chasing after butterflies and a scolding jay, she found a hidden tangle of vines within the forest. Soon it became an enchanted place that beckoned to her in among the leaves, blossoms, and luscious fruit. Her fear had melted away as she felt comforted by the solitude of this natural island within the island. Eventually, Auntie Beth found her skipping along the path home, never knowing the silent bond Martha had formed here with Noepe. Her entire life, body and soul, was grounded by the peace and tranquility of her special little vineyard.

Martha was constantly guarded by her dog — Argon, a muscular Mastiff mix with intelligent eyes and a trot that resembled a draft horse. No one was quite sure exactly what kind of dog he was, but Martha claimed he came from a trade ship bound for New Amsterdam. She'd first seen him as a pup near the wharf, nosing at a half-split barrel painted with a faded coat of arms — a gold beast rearing on its hind legs. The letters beneath curled like little waves: Compagnia di… Ar-gon. She had sounded it out under her breath, slow and careful, letting the strange but important-sounding word roll in her mouth. Argon. It seemed like the type of name a great foreign king might give to his bravest knight. He was a watcher like Martha, and seemed to understand her in a way people often didn't. His sensitive ears flicked toward every rustle in the brush.

Argon nosed along the wall, his coat catching the light in rusty-gold threads. He paused now and then to listen — ears tilting, nostrils flaring — before circling back to Martha's side. She set down her basket and began her morning rounds, checking knots, pinching away the small shoots that stole strength from the fruiting stems. Her hands knew the work so well that her thoughts wandered, unbidden, to the sound of bees murmuring in the warm air.

When the wild vines were trimmed into place and pesky weeds taken care of, Martha counted the clusters eager to ripen. These would be too early for the harvest, but perfect for juice the villagers so often enjoyed. She gathered her basket and gardening knife then sat for a moment on the stone wall where it warmed in the dappled sunlight.

A shimmer caught her eye — no more than sunlight wavering through leaves — yet her breath slowed, her vision sharpened. The hum of bees deepened, the air thickened, and the hollow seemed to hold its breath. She saw, as if from a great distance, a figure: a girl in a coarse shift, head bent, arms drawn forward as though pulled by invisible currents. Dust swirled about her bare feet. Martha recognized her. The African girl from the orphanage she called "Daisy".

The girl's face turned, just enough for their eyes to meet across the dreamy gulf that lay between them. Her mouth formed Martha's name — or maybe only a cry. The vision wavered, then broke apart like mist. Bees droned again; leaves flickered; the air moved. The specter of Daisy was gone.

Martha rose and stood for a long moment, hand on a grapevine, the rough bark grounding her. She did not ask herself if she'd imagined it — the island had its own ways of speaking. For a heartbeat, Martha still felt the orphanage walls pressing in on her, though she had never slept beneath its roof. She remembered the rows of narrow cots, the children's faces flickering in and out of her memory like candle flames. Some had been taken away by families and never returned; others simply vanished, their absence spoken of only in whispers. Daisy had been the smallest of them, always with dreamy eyes too big for her face, and now here she was again—summoned to her mind from the shadows of that place. The thought chilled Martha more than the vision itself.

She picked up her basket and moved on, Argon pacing her steps, the sound of his paws soft against the damp earth.

Before leaving, she crouched beside the old wall and tugged free a small wooden box hidden in the hollow. She opened it with care, adding the **wampompeag** beads she had found to her secret collection: a tarnished silver coin, loose pages from a book with faded illustrations, an osprey feather, and tiny wood carvings Tobiasquash had shaped for her. Beneath them lay a picture of Jesus, the dark eyes and outstretched arms calling to mind the painted crucifixion she once saw on Caroline's wall.

As a child, the figure had filled her with fear — the nails, the blood, the twisted anguish too heavy for her to imagine. But now, staring at the worn page, something new stirred: not only the pain, but the sense that someone could choose such suffering out of love. She didn't fully understand it, yet the thought pressed against her heart like a truth waiting to be known.

Closing the lid, she tucked the box back into its hiding place. Before leaving, she crouched beside the old wall, rolled a heavy stone into place and drew vines across the top, leaving no sign of the narrow footpath she alone knew.

The path from her vineyard to the lane wound between stone walls overgrown with beach plum and wild rose. Martha kept one hand on Argon's back as they walked, his fur still warm from the sunlit garden. The scent of crushed grape leaves clung to her skin, a reminder of the place she had left behind — the one place on the island that felt wholly her own, beyond the reach of judging minds.

Out on the open lane, the eyes of the world returned. Some belonged to people she knew, others to those who only thought they knew her. She was used to the glance that lingered a heartbeat too long, weighing whether she belonged to one side or the other: Wampanoag or European. It made her stand straighter without meaning to, as though her spine knew before her mind that she was both, and neither, and something else entirely.

Argon's steady gait matched her own. He didn't care which world claimed her. But he noticed moods the way other dogs noticed rabbits. Sometimes his ears twitched toward a sound she couldn't yet hear; sometimes his shoulder brushed her hip like an anchor. He had done that even before the vineyard became hers.

She had learned that it was easier to let others decide what they thought she was — until they were wrong about something that mattered. Then she would speak, not loudly, but in a way that made them stop and listen. She didn't call it leadership, and wouldn't have recognized the word in herself if someone else had used it. To her, it was simply being true to herself in the most natural way.

The low hum of voices drifted from the meadow ahead — a rhythm of work song over the rustle of corn stalks being harvested. Martha's pace slowed. The morning's stillness had left her with the strange aftertaste of that vision in the garden, and the memory of Daisy's face in it made her skin prickle. Argon felt it too; his head came up, ears pricked.

As they neared a curve in the lane, a faint cloud of dust hung in the air, kicked up by the feet of those working the rows. She could already make out the silhouettes: bent backs, swaying arms, baskets swinging. The work was steady, almost graceful, until it wasn't.

Ahead, rows of cornfields stretched toward the edge of the forest, and among them, groups of enslaved field workers moved rhythmically in the morning light. The women and children bent low, husking or weeding. The men dragged crates toward a waiting cart

Martha's chest tightened, but she kept walking, her eyes forward, Argon matched her stride — as if they both knew that stepping toward trouble too quickly would draw it closer.

She walked the edge of the lane, careful not to draw too much attention, but her eyes scanned the workers. She saw Daisy — in person now — just a bit younger than herself, her dark braids swinging as she worked. The two had shared whispered games at the orphanage in the past, exchanged a berry here, a flower there. Daisy looked up just long enough to spot her. She gave a sheepish little wave — quickly silenced by a barked command from the overseer.

Argon's ears flattened.

A teenage boy, older and strong for his age, had lifted his head too long. The overseer, a red-faced man with a rawhide whip curled at his belt, stepped forward and barked, "You there — eyes down, boy!"

But it wasn't the boy he moved toward — it was Martha.

"You! Girl! Get over here!" he yelled. "Let's see if you're so proud when you've done a day's work!"

Argon growled deep and menacing as he stepped between Martha and the path into the field. His hackles raised. The overseer paused mid-stride and reconsidered his actions. He swiped a fly from his nose and coughed nervously.

Martha stepped back, hand resting gently on Argon's head. Her spine was straight. She didn't speak — not to a field overseer. Not to him. The moment stretched tight, strained like a ship's line in the wind.

The tyrant tapped the whip at his side, sneered, then turned back toward the workers. "Your day will come, half-breed." he muttered loud enough for her to hear. But he didn't come closer.

Martha exhaled and gave Argon a quick scratch behind the ear. "You always know, don't you?" she whispered.

From the fields, the quiet sound of a work song rose again — a slow, mournful melody sung by the women. Daisy glanced once more over her shoulder and offered the smallest nod.

Martha walked on.

She turned toward the wooded bend, the morning light broke through the trees in scattered shards. The lane narrowed here, growing wild with sweet fern and bayberry. Martha heard rustling in the bushes.

"RRAAAAAWWGGFF!"

Tobiasquash leaped from behind a bush with a wild, awkward snarl, limbs flailing like an uncoiled spring. He was tall and lean, his brown skin sun-darkened to match his eyes. He kept his shoulder length hair tied with a strip of cloth. Her cousin was full Wampanoag and full of mischief.

Martha jumped back — half in shock, half in delight — Argon lunged forward with a snap but stopped himself just in time. The boy laughed and threw his arms up in surrender.

"You nearly got your leg bitten off, you fool," Martha said, breathing hard.

"Môsi, you still scream like the **wusqôhs** — rabbit!" the boy said, grinning.

"I did not scream." she muttered, brushing off her dress.

"I'm helping you stay sharp." he laughed.

Argon finally relaxed, sniffing the boy's leg with practiced disdain. Tobiasquash gave him a scratch behind the ear, which was begrudgingly accepted.

"Where are you headed?" he asked.

"Tending to the vines. Auntie Beth needs plenty of grapes for her dyes, and she says she "only has two hands" so I help as best I can." She explained, "Come with me Tobi. You can help too."

"Oh no . . . I'm not going to get tangled in that." He replied quickly, "I'm a scouting for my father's hunting party."

"Making all this noise?" She teased. "You're just scaring the **ahtuck** farther away."

Tobiasquash grinned, but there was a quick glance over his shoulder before he spoke again. "That **Tawasquat** was asking about you yesterday," he said, drawing out the name like it was bait.

Martha narrowed her eyes, "And?"

He shrugged, pretending to study the ground. "She

wanted to know why I spend time with that girl and the "ghost woman."'"

Martha felt her cheeks warm, though from anger or embarrassment, she wasn't sure.

"I told her that I'd rather keep company with clever ghosts than dull fish," Tobiasquash said, flashing his teeth. "She didn't like that."

Martha gave a snort despite herself. Argon pressed close to her leg, tail flicking once before settling again.

Tobiasquash play-acted a serious hand signal to someone in the woods, then bounded off silently as a cat. She laughed out loud and called after him, "There's no one there, you pesky **sôtyum**!"

As Martha continued on, an inner vibration came to her like a trusted spark of knowing. Her grin faded slightly as a thought slipped into her mind: "It does feel like there's someone watching nearby."

Argon's ears pricked up and he sniffed the air.

"You feel it too, don't you boy." She patted him on the back.

Martha glanced toward the trees. Her skin prickled again, though she couldn't say why. Somewhere in the woods beyond the bend, her father Pashanok was watching.

— *Chapter 3* —

Argon jumped to attention outside the cottage, focused on someone walking through the garden.

"Alloo? Alloo?"

The voice was pinched and soft—meant to sound friendly, but a little strained, like the speaker was always listening more than talking.

Argon's growl melted into a soft howl; his tail began to wag. He trotted outside as their neighbor stepped into view, a knitting basket swinging from one hand and a morsel of jerky in the other.

"Good morning, Miss Beth," their distant neighbor, the widow Lydia sang out, all faux cheer as she fed Argon his treat. "I thought I'd bring this dress hem I've botched beyond hope—and oh, such a morning for a walk!"

Beth turned slowly, she swept her gauze veil a little higher, a little tighter across her face. "Come in, Miss Webb," she said kindly. "Let's see what mischief your hem has been up to."

Martha, already sweeping near the door, stiffened as the young widow stepped inside. The woman's eyes scanned the room like a hawk—taking in the kettle, the wool hanging to dry, the threadbare curtains, the faint trace of lavender soap. Her gaze lingered just long enough to leave a film of judgment.

Beth held up the hem and clicked her tongue. "No great crime here."

"Oh, you're too kind," said Lydia, already moving toward the back window, turning to Martha. "I passed some Wampanoag boys out by the bend. One might've been your—ah—cousin?"

Beth gave a look to Martha who turned her attention to Argon.

"And I hear there's a ship just come in," the woman added. "Saw the sails in the harbor at dawn. Strange-looking crew, someone said. Came in on the tide."

"Did they now?" Beth replied mildly, her hand folding the hem just so.

"Yes. And the Reverend's son is back, they say." She leaned forward. "Do you think he'll visit?"

Beth smiled sweetly. "Only if he needs a sail or net mended."

Lydia pursed her lips, sensing her moment had passed. "Well! I should let you get to your wool. These dyes look like a handful."

"No need to rush, Ms. Lydia." Beth said, gently guiding her toward the door. "Have a good day."

Martha watched her leave, wondering how a person deserving compassion could drive it from her heart so easily.

Once the latch clicked behind her, Beth let out a long sigh and lowered her veil. The smallpox scars beneath were startling, even in the soft light—pitted skin along her right cheek and jaw, her lower eyelid pulled slightly downward as if she had suffered a stroke. Her hair, once a beautiful auburn, had gone a ghostly white.

Martha didn't flinch. "She finds excuses to visit so she can make up stories for her friends, Muttie" she said, another attempt at calling Auntie Beth "mother". This time in German, heard in town recently. Beth gave her a stern look that quickly melted to a smile.

"Oh my sweet little dove. I know." Beth responded, touching her face gently, "That is the nature of fear. They fear anyone different, like us — independent and free — so they think we are trouble. Stories are more interesting than the dull reality of truth."

"I don't care what they think." Martha insisted.

Beth shook her head. "Their thoughts will someday turn to actions, Martha. We must care about that."

"But —." Martha softly protested.

Beth nodded towards the space Lydia had just left as she rolled the diaphanous material around her neck. "I know the names they call me because of my hair and these smallpox scars."

"That is so unfair!" Martha stomped her foot, "I will tell them the truth to make them stop!"

"I know, my love. But you have to understand. You are an orphan, Martha. You cannot call me "Muttie" or "Mother". We are not like a normal family. When you were a baby, Caroline and your mother insisted I take you from the orphanage for your protection. I can't explain everything right now, but you'll see the wisdom of our caution over time."

They worked in silence for a while, folding wool and setting skeins to dry. Argon pawed at the door, anxious to go out. Beth handed Martha a cloth-wrapped parcel bound with hemp twine. "This is for Mr. Durand."

Martha carried it along with an armful of other things to the cart outside. She found Moses, their black and white goat grazing on dandelions near the path and fitted the harness over his back. With a few more flowers and a little coaxing, she led him to the cart.

"We're loaded and ready to go." Martha called in the door.

Beth inspected the contents, tightened a strap on the cart, and gave Moses a pat. She set the strap down and reached for the last bundle. Martha adjusted a basket inside so it wouldn't jostle while Argon paced near the doorway, tail brushing the wood in a steady rhythm.

"Please fetch my blue shawl from the peg." Beth called over her shoulder, "We're going into the village on business, and I won't have us looking out of place."

"And the merchant list?" Martha waved a small slate over her head.

"Yes. Dock Street today," Auntie Beth nodded, then with a knowing wink to Argon, "Let's see what trouble you'll find this time."

Moses bleated his complaints as they started off, his tail wagging with emotion. Beth tapped the cart every so often to keep him moving. Argon padded ahead and looked back, his watchful eyes naturally alert to anything out of place.

Martha hesitated a while before speaking. "Tobi says Tawasquat's been asking about me."

Beth glanced up, her face unreadable. "Oh?"

"She asked him why he spends time with 'that girl' and her 'ghost mother.'" Martha kept her tone light, but her hands gripped the basket a little tighter.

Beth straightened slowly, the leather strap in her hands creaking. "Ghost mother, is it? That's a step up from 'plague ghost' or 'witch', I suppose."

Martha tried to smother a smile, but it came through anyway. "You're not bothered?"

Beth's eyes softened, though her mouth stayed firm. "I'm bothered if it makes you a target. Now, do you see why I guard against being called your mother? Names and labels are meant to stick, whether they belong or not. People have long memories for simple things they never truly knew, and short patience for what they don't want to know. You're already walking a road most wouldn't understand. I'd hate to think I've made it rougher."

"You haven't, Auntie Beth" Martha said quickly. "It's just talk."

Beth searched her face, then nodded once. "Words have teeth, Martha. Just remember, you choose which ones to listen for—and why."

The slow trip into the small village of Great Harbor was a pleasant adventure. They passed under massive oaks as a herd of deer grazed in the distance while flicking their white tails, wary of Argon's scent. A lone osprey screeched from above. The lane wound past fields still wet with morning dew, through woods where wild raspberries and grape vines tangled in the underbrush.

As they passed a mossy graveyard, Beth slowed to a stop. Argon noticed the hesitation before Martha and stood in front of the goat cart, halting their progress. Beth paused at the low stone wall, one hand on the gate. Martha lingered just outside, Argon sniffed among the lichen covered stones. The graves here were mostly new, the names barely worn by salt and wind.

Beth's gaze was fixated on the brightest gravestone among the Mayhew plot. It simply read, "Caroline Mayhew – Loving wife and mother" Her tears came freely, draining the heaviness from her heart. The death of her best friend and mentor, a kindred soul for the ages, was still a fresh wound to her heart despite the years gone by. Caroline Mayhew had been the only woman Beth ever trusted, the one who tended to her secret pregnancy. When Martha was born, she saved them both in ways no one on the island ever fully knew.

Martha lingered beside her, the name Caroline stirring only the faintest memories — a gentle voice that soothed her to sleep, and the scent of lilacs that always seemed to follow.

Beth stood very still, head bowed, and Martha waited, not wanting to interrupt. While she waited, her gaze wandered. A smaller stone nearby had caught her eye, half-hidden by ivy. She leaned closer, more curious than thoughtful. It read:

'Martha'

That was all.

No other name she recognized. No dates she cared to puzzle out. Just the name itself, worn smooth by weather and time. Argon's tail brushed once against her leg. Martha straightened and stepped back toward Beth, the name still a bit tight in her chest — warm with sympathy, and a small, unspoken relief that it was not her time, as Auntie Beth would say. She felt awkward for a moment, then quickly strode over to give Beth a hug.

Beth stopped her with a quick gesture and said, "Don't look now, but the trees have eyes."

Argon was looking for both of them.

On the far side of the graveyard, two figures slowed their walk. Miriam Blodgett, her shawl tight around her shoulders, leaned toward Abner Pease, a wiry man with a fisherman's gait.

"That's the one," Miriam murmured. "The woman is a witch, so Lydia says. Lives with the girl in that shack down by the forest path."

Abner squinted toward the wall. "And what business has she in the graveyard?"

"Best not to ask," Miriam said, glancing over her shoulder. "Best not to cross her, either, by Jove."

Beth rose, brushing her hands against her skirt. The wind carried their voices just enough for Martha to hear the edge in them. She felt Argon press close to her leg, as if he'd heard it too.

Beth closed the gate with a quiet click, her expression unreadable. "Time to get moving. We've got a long day ahead."

She waved her hands forward to move them along. Then to herself quietly, "Times I wish it were me there instead of you my beautiful Caroline, you were such an amazing soul." Wiping the last tear from her eye, she put her hand on Martha's shoulder to reassure the kind-hearted girl.

As they neared the village, the trees fell away to reveal Great Harbor spread before them in the bright salt air. Morning light spilled across the water, turning the ripples in the bay to quicksilver. The tide rocked the swaying ships, their massive hulls anchored like floating islands in an ocean of currents. Along the waterfront, gulls wheeled and cried over the fish sheds while the mingled voices of English, Portuguese, and Wampanoag rose and fell with the rhythm of the waves. Smoke curled lazily from village chimneys, drifting above thatched rooftops weathered in soft grays.

A few English families strolled together along Water Street with other passengers who had disembarked from *The Deliverance*, a newly arrived ship from London. Their city formal attire stood out among the villagers and merchants, frilled cuffs and collars, powdered wigs and painted faces. One wealthy family clustered together nervously protecting the bags they carried. The daughter was about Martha's age in a white dress with a red ribbon in her hair. The mother wore a blue satin dress and twirled her white lace parasol; absentmindedly humming a sailors' shanty tune to herself.

The girl pointed at Auntie Beth and blurted out, "Oh Mummy! Is she . . . one of them?" She made a show jumping back behind her parents, then whispered loudly, "A witch?"

The mother turned scarlet and tugged her daughter along. Beth said nothing. The girl turned and pointed at Martha's dress with a sneer, "Look at the rags she's wearing!"

Martha froze, then with wild eyes she barked

"**nôônâmês**!" in Wampanoag. A nearby islander recognized the slight and laughed, spitting into the sand.

Beth and Martha turned toward Dock Street. Overhead, the Union Jack above the Mayhews' make-shift custom house rustled like dry leaves.

Argon barked once, uneasy. Martha looked up. "*Something feels different.*" she murmured to herself.

Flags and sails snapped in unison. The air carried a sharper edge now, smelling faintly of rain far out to sea. Somewhere along the wharf, a loose halyard began clanging against its mast.

The wind had changed.

— Chapter 4 —

Along Dock Street, the day had already begun in earnest. Shopkeepers swung their shutters open to reveal neat rows of goods — bolts of cloth, barrels of molasses, jars of spice — while sailors shouldered coils of rope and crates of cargo from ship to warehouse.

The masts in the harbor stood like a forest stripped of leaves, their rigging humming in the breeze. Gulls wheeled overhead, their cries sharp as they dove to snatch scraps from the fishmonger's cart. The air was rich with the mingled scents of tarred rope, fresh bread from the baker's oven, and the briny tang of the tide rolling in.

Sailors and passengers from a local packet ship stretched their legs on the cobblestones, some craning their necks at the unfamiliar skyline of new construction, others heading straight for the taverns and shops. Children darted between barrels and wagon wheels, chasing each other through the clamor, their laughter blending with the slap of water against the pilings.

Beth guided Moses and his cart along beside the bustling villagers, her pace steady. Martha kept pace at her side, Argon trotting just ahead, ears flicking at the shouts of sailors and the crack of a whip somewhere down the street. This was the heart of Great Harbor, a village that seemed to expand with every new ship's arrival. It was busy, loud, and unyielding. Though it never stopped to make room for them, neither did it turn them away.

Just then, Edgar Vincent appeared by Mr. Gunton's German bakery, brushing flour from his shirt. "Miss Martha," he grinned. "Thought I might find you here."

"You did," she said dryly. "I am not found."

Martha remembered the first time she had met him—Edgar Vincent, thin but stretching taller each season, the golden-haired banker's son in fine linen trousers soiled at the knees. She had been lost in a drift of beach roses, their perfume holding her still when his shadow fell across her. Martha turned quickly, startled by this jaunty boy with his hands on his hips. Edgar studied her with unguarded curiosity, then smiled, boyish and bold.

"Our eyes," he said, tilting his head, "they're the same color blue."

It unnerved her, the heat that rose in her chest—her first flutter of feeling toward a boy. Yet the moment soured as quickly as it bloomed, for he added with careless wonder, "Strange, though, for a girl who looks so… native."

The sting stayed, but so too did the memory of his noticing her, a mixture she could never quite set aside.

He began walking beside them until another village boy called out a tease to the banker's son, "Edgar! Mind your place!"

Red-faced, he veered away.

Martha shrugged as she exchanged glances with Auntie Beth who couldn't help but smile and shake her head. Argon stopped. His ears pricked as his gaze curiously focused on a space between two buildings. Moses halted their cart, stubbornly refusing to continue as a horse whinnied in alarm.

With a loud crash and bang, a mostly naked little boy came running and screaming from the alley between the fishmonger's and Chandler's provision store. He made a straight bee-line to Martha where he begged her to help him, "She's going to kill me! She's going to kill me, Martha! Help!"

The sailors and townspeople paused to watch the drama with curiosity. He clung to Martha's leg with determined desperation. Poor little Charlie—all of six years old, with tears streaking down his dusty face—blubbered on her clean dress, "Please, don't let them take me back! I'll be good — I'll work, I'll clean, anything you want!"

"Get back here immediately, you little cur!" Miss Hawkins, the grizzled headmaster of the orphanage, waved a leather strap as she marched down the street with two older teen boys. "You will have that washing if I must drown you to do it, so help me Lord!"

Charlie clung to Martha, his little hands pinching at her leg like lobster claws. He wiped his muddy cheek on her dress and appealed to her with pleading eyes. "Save me, Martha!"

Miss Hawkins advanced in formation with her young wards as if she was leading a British regiment into battle; each marching step displayed her militant demeanor.

Argon began to growl as the fur stood up on his back, teeth starting to bare.

Beth led Moses and the cart a few steps to block

Miss Hawkin's direct assault and said, "Good morning Hazel. Such a beautiful day for a stroll in town, isn't it?"

"Don't interfere with my official business, woman!" she glared at Beth. "Just because the late Mrs. Mayhew doted on you doesn't give you any right to deny my authority! Now step aside!"

She turned to one of the older boys. "Oliver, take this little rat over to the horse trough and give him the dunking he deserves. Look at all that filth!"

The older boy gave a wicked sneer and waved a stiff-bristled brush at Charlie.

Charlie shivered with fear and yelped at the thought.

Ignoring Miss Hawkins' overbearing demands, Beth responded by addressing Charlie in a clear, kind voice. "Well now young man, I see you're determined to clean yourself with miss Martha's dress, now aren't you? Let's just take a minute to finish the job with this cloth I have here."

She began to wipe the tears mixed with dust and dirt from his face. After a few swipes she handed the cloth to Oliver and told him to go soak it in the trough water.

Miss Hawkins folded her arms and glared at Charlie, "What she doesn't clean, I will!"

A young English couple with their children took special interest in this little confrontation to the chagrin of the Headmistress. She halted her tirade but maintained her commanding posture. Oliver looked to Miss Hawkins for direction and she reluctantly nodded.

Argon broke the tension with a deep guttural bark! He stood between the Headmistress and his pack of humans.

Miss Hawkins, unnerved by Beth's unexpectedly reasoned resistance said, "You keep that untethered brute away from me! He's a danger to our peaceful town and I won't stand for it!"

Martha had a lot to say in response to that but held her tongue after Auntie Beth gave her a look.

Oliver returned with the dripping cloth and tossed it at Martha, hoping to hit her unawares. She caught it mid-air, then bent down on one knee and softly wiped Charlie's face. She whispered a few things in his ear to which he nodded, then turned to Beth and said, "We need help with our work in town, don't we Auntie?"

Beth caught the meaning of her request and agreed. "Hazel. I'm sure there are many more things you'd rather attend to than this dirty little mouse. May we take him for the morning and return him in sparkling condition?"

The confrontation had passed, and Miss Hawkins knew she'd left the orphanage in haste chasing down the errant boy. Who knew what trouble the other children were causing in her absence even with Ms. Mitchell there?

"His labor isn't free, Beth. I expect two pence upon his return, or can't you afford that?"

"I value his help, Hazel. You will have your payment," Beth replied.

"Come on boys." Miss Hazel Hawkins abruptly turned away and quickly marched back down the alley she emerged from, Oliver and his friend reluctantly in tow.

Charlie heaved a heavy sigh and hugged Martha all over again. He lunged toward Beth who caught him at arm's length saying, "No. No. I'll give no hugs until your little hide is fully dirt free!"

People returned to their business, and the young English man approached Beth holding out a few pence. His gaze flicked between her and Martha. "Your daughter?"

"No, sir." Beth adjusted her veil. "A friend's child."

"I was saving this as a donation to the orphanage anyway, so giving it to you now is a convenience for me. I trust you will conduct your business honestly."

Beth couldn't resist and accepted his generosity. "That I will sir, on my honor."

He turned to his son, very close to Charlie's size and age. "Is there anything you could offer to these people, Arthur? Anything at all?"

Arthur felt embarrassed by the sudden attention, looked at his feet and shrugged bashfully.

"What about those britches you claim to have outgrown?"

His wife gave him a wide-eyed look and pursed her lips. She took her daughter by the hand, "Charlotte. Let's leave your father to his charity work." They abruptly walked away.

The Englishman waved to the ship's mate who was directing sailors about the dock. "Sir! A moment sir!"

In no time at all, little Charlie was scrubbed clean and outfitted with a pair of fairly used britches and Martha's little ensemble carried on with a new member in tow. He seemed to attract dirt with each step though, and she had to ward him off every time he tried to ride Argon.

Martha and Auntie Beth stopped their cart full of wares near the main dock and set a few items out on display. Beth pulled out a worn parasol to shade herself from the sun while Martha took a pre-wrapped parcel tied with yarn and left to deliver it to Mr. Chandler's store. It wasn't a coincidence that Edgar spent much of his time there, although the bakery was his favorite place by choice. His father and Mr. Chandler were in business together.

Beth balanced a wrapped bundle in her arms as she entered the finely stocked shop of Francois Durand, a well-known cloth merchant whose pride in quality was surpassed only by his pride in heritage. His powdered wig was set a touch askew today, perhaps from a morning nap, and the ruffles at his wrist were dramatically flared like a sea captain in port.

"Ah, madame," he called, waving them in with one hand while fussing with a bolt of indigo linen in the other. "You are always punctual — and that I admire more than any hemline."

Beth smiled graciously and set the bundle on the counter. "Three repaired jackets, cleaned and mended. And I believe the apron with the wine stain is back to life."

Francois lifted the fabric with reverence. "C'est magnifique." He ran his fingers along the stitching, then clapped his hands. "Monique! Come see the work of your favorite island sorceress!"

From behind a doorway curtain stepped Monique Durand, all ribbons and curiosity, no more than thirteen. She carried herself with the dramatic poise only a girl with an artistic father could learn. Her eyes lit up when she saw Martha. The two would be good friends during different times, but even now they were happy acquaintances.

"You embroidered these grapes?" Monique asked, running her fingers across the edge of Martha's sleeve.

Martha nodded sheepishly. "Just to cover a stain. It wasn't anything."

"It's beautiful," Monique said, brushing a bit of dried mud near the hem. "A shame about these, though." She glanced up with a teasing smile, nodding towards Charlie who was fidgeting with spools of thread, "What happened? Did someone blow their nose on you?"

Martha looked down at the faint marks left by his tear-streaked hands. "Something like that," she murmured, but smiled.

Monique stepped closer and leaned toward the front window, then back toward Martha. "That boy outside… the one with the sandy hair and soft boots? He's been watching you from across the street." She raised her eyebrows and nodded slyly.

Martha's cheeks turned a quick shade of rose.

"I knew it!" Monique whispered, beaming.

Before Martha could answer, she glanced out the window — and saw nothing. Edgar had vanished, just a drift of dust and sunlight where he'd stood.

Beth finished her exchange with Francois, who slipped a few extra coins onto the table with a wink. "You did more than promised, madame. As always."

They exited into the afternoon air, Charlie now at Martha's side, playing with a little ball of twine he found. His face was cleaner now, and his eyes darted from one storefront to the next with curiosity instead of fear.

Their next stop was a cobbler's shed run by Mr. Mitchell, where Beth had left a boot sole to be patched. Outside, Reverend Mayhew held court as a debate brewed between him and a pair of town elders — one a Whig, the other a self-styled Royalist — leaning against a pickle barrel. The Reverend was a stocky Englishman with a penchant for intellectual arguments and political issues. His green eyes flashed with excitement as he quoted scripture and law, always arguing for "peace and security between men of good will". No one could match his memory or reasoning. The villagers of Great Harbor had created the position of Constable just for him, and he in turn created the Custom House to assure all trade was legal and fair.

"I assure you, gentlemen," the Reverend said with both conviction and polish, "there is only one true divine king — Jesus Christ."

The Royalist scoffed, but Mayhew softened. "Whose Kingdom, of course, is the Heavens. We may differ here on Earth, but our souls are bound elsewhere."

Beth nodded to him respectfully as she entered the shop.

He turned and addressed Charlie with a smile. "Young man. Shall I walk you back to your post at the orphanage? I imagine Miss Hawkins is searching the shadows by now."

Before Charlie could reply, Martha gave his arm a gentle pat.

"Charlie," she said warmly, like a doting older sister, "you've been such a great help today. We couldn't have managed without your strong muscles and extra energy."

Charlie's face lit up like lantern glass. He puffed his chest and gave a comic little salute.

"Yes, Mum! Charlie Porter, at your service anytime!"

Reverend Mayhew raised an eyebrow at Charlie's

phrasing. "Yes, Mum," he repeated with a chuckle. "We men have important work to do."

As the Reverend turned with the boy and began down the lane, Charlie's concerned voice piped up behind him:

"We do? What work do we have to do next?"

The Reverend laughed—a warm, full sound—and ruffled the boy's hair.

Beth watched them go in silence, her expression unreadable. Then she gently turned Moses' cart back toward the lane and nodded to Martha.

"Time to be heading home."

And for just a moment, the road ahead felt as safe as the road behind.

— *Chapter 5* —

As Beth led the way back down Dock Street, her senses pricked without warning. A threatening energy filled the air like the pressure of a new and different storm. No one else seemed to notice—except Martha. She shot a look to Auntie Beth that silently asked, *"What is this feeling?"*

A newly arrived merchant ship was tied at the end of the longest pier—black-hulled, with a rake to her bow that made her look restless even at anchor: The *Deliverance*. Sailors swarmed her decks, coiling lines, shouting orders, running out the gangway. The creak of block and tackle, the slap of canvas, and the distant ring of a ship's bell mingled with the bustle ashore.

Auntie Beth responded to Martha with the tiniest shake of her head, then cocked it ever so slightly toward the far end of Dock Street. Martha understood the signal. She gathered Moses' lead and turned the cart to follow Beth without a word. Argon stiffened, his eyes fixated on Martha's alarmed expression. Her senses on high alert, she searched every sight, sound and scent. Then she heard it, a man's voice. It was unmistakably forceful. That steady, low tone like the rumble of a rock-slide. The hard-edged syllables—k, t, and the disturbing snake-like s.

On the partially built wharf, carts and barrows trundled past, their wheels grinding on the cobblestones. A wagon of fish barrels gave off a sharp tang that clung to the air. Passengers from the ship wove through the crowd, casting curious glances at the newcomer in the harbor—and at the man now striding down the gangway with a boy at his heels, both dressed for travel, both carrying the kind of confidence that pushed the street aside without a word.

Lord Goodwin Morgrave stood in command as if it were his divine right, his shock of red hair and piercing gray eyes drew the attention he secretly craved. He stood tall for a man of average height, his thin stature belied the strength of his weathered physique. Lord Morgrave was the kind of man who laughed, not at some joke or jest, but at the pain and fear of his prey. And that laugh now sounded across the harbor. It started as a light childish giggle and built into a low derisive guffaw that broadcast to every ear on Dock Street.

Beth had heard it before. The voice conjured up long suppressed nightmares from her youth; the torment of her escape on that Atlantic crossing so many years ago. Her soul reacted instinctively. She felt her knees weaken; her lip quivered the tiniest bit.

Martha started toward Beth, but she waved her off with a heavy whisper, "Stay calm, dear. Follow me."

Beth turned and walked on as if nothing were wrong. Martha fell in step beside her.

"Why am I feeling this way?" she whispered. "*What's going on?*"

Beth didn't answer. She simply nodded toward a nearby shop where coils of rope were stacked in all sizes.

Martha slipped behind a hand-painted sign to hide and peered back down Dock Street, looking for the man to match the voice. She nearly jumped out of her skin when Beth placed a hand on her shoulder.

Beth pointed to the cart and said in her usual merchant tone, "Would you please hand that worsted wool sample to me, dear?"

Then, more quietly:

"Gather Argon. Hold the cart steady. Everything will be alright."

Martha did as she was told, moving in a trance of worry and confusion. Her eyes scanned the street, searching for the source of Beth's fear.

A group of sailors lounged nearby, joking and jeering in the way idle men often did. They mocked the town's patchwork harbor, pointing at the half-built stone wharf and the temporary dock worn from over-use. A ship's captain stood nearby in discussion with a merchant, inspecting a small mountain of supplies for inventory.

"Captain Drake!" Lord Morgrave's voice cracked through the air like a cannon shot.

Argon jumped. The goat bleated in alarm. Martha's breath hitched.

She couldn't make out the words, but the tone that followed—hissing and snapping—was unmistakably cruel. The voice seized the captain with the merciless grip of an osprey's talons.

Sailors scattered. Barrels were moved, casks shifted—anything for them to appear busy.

"You!" A hand shot out—two of the fingers partially missing.

"And you three! Yes, YOU. Get over here and heft these trunks to the inn!"

The sailors looked to the captain in hesitation.

He nodded grimly, too tired to argue. He'd had just about enough of Lord Goodwin Morgrave—self-styled Royal Bounty Hunter with a lust for power. The man had been a curse from the moment he stepped aboard in London. Now, with only days left between Great Harbor and New Amsterdam, the captain prayed the voyage would end without blood.

Martha slipped back inside the store. Beth had returned to her full business stature, holding a deep purple bolt of wool in her arms. The merchant waved her off.

"No call for that shade, miss. Purple is for the field folk and Wampanoags."

Beth raised an eyebrow. "This shade is the island's signature on the seven seas. It rises in value every season. Isn't that right, Mrs. Dunlay?"

A sea captain's wife standing nearby, nodded in agreement.

They danced the customary steps of a trade negotiation, but Martha's eyes stayed fixed beyond the shop's doorway.

The man with the cruel voice paced Dock Street with a leather-bound ledger tucked under one arm and a riding crop in the other. His red hair burned in the sun like a flame licking at the wind. When any man slowed or hesitated, the crop cracked by his hands like fire across dry twigs. Though a donkey cart sat idle nearby, Lord Morgrave insisted the sailors carry every trunk by hand. He marched ahead like a field marshal, dragging his conscripts behind. Those of lower stature he glared aside. Those of means received a polished hat-tip—his smile chilling in its civility.

Once she spotted Lord Morgrave, Martha couldn't look away. Her whole body tensed with the stillness of a rabbit hiding from a predator. Something deep inside her warned—Look away! But it was too late. As if by some spell she was frozen in place. His eyes locked with hers.

One side of his mouth curled into a smile that never reached his eyes.

Then, to her horror, he began walking toward her—his gait softening, his face now warm and open, like an old friend returning home. Before he could reach her though, a new voice broke the spell.

"Ah! You must be one of the gentleman just arrived on the *Deliverance*!" Reverend Mayhew called out for all to hear. He recognized Lord Morgrave as a man of the world and intercepted him at the edge of the shop's boardwalk, introducing himself as the village constable.

Lord Goodwin Morgrave was affronted by the Reverend's seemingly ignorant interjection. Eyeing his clerical attire, Morgrave fell into his routine social greeting, despite his irritation, held out his hand and said, "Good day, Reverend. Lord Goodwin Morgrave, humble servant of the King. How do you do?"

"Very well, thank you." He replied, "As town Constable and Custom House Officer, I just have a few questions to ask . . . "

Martha stepped back, slipped inside, and flashed Beth a warning hand signal. Beth turned, recognized the shift in tone, and gently folded her fabric with care. She didn't look back toward the harbor, but her hand closed tight around the edge of her veil. She knew the storm had come to shore.

Outside, Mayhew launched into questions about the voyage, the weather, and Lord Morgrave's purpose on the island.

By the time Martha dared peek back through the doorway, both men had moved on—walking together up Water Street toward the center of town, their voices fading as they went. Just behind them, the ship's boy followed within earshot.

Skip Frey was the kind of boy always helpful to Morgrave, especially when no one was watching. He was no older than fourteen, with shaggy curls and a face so common it was utterly forgettable. He grinned at everyone knowingly, like a friend. Too easily. Too often.

He watched the scene unfold between Morgrave and Mayhew with quiet amusement, then drifted away from the road without anyone noticing. One moment he was there, the next he was gone—vanishing like smoke into a crack between buildings.

No one saw his slight figure slink into the shadows except for Lord Morgrave. Without turning, he tilted his head ever so slightly—acknowledging the boy's near invisible presence.

A short walk from the merchant stalls, a trio of village boys lingered at the dock's edge, legs dangling just above the tide. One of them — fair-haired and lightly freckled — held a crooked fishing pole and squinted into the midday sun. Edgar, local and likable, was known more for his clever tongue than his casting skills.

Skip saw an opportunity for mischief he couldn't resist. The posture, the boots, the faint shine of good cloth beneath the dirt. Not a nobleman's son — no — but a merchant's boy. Comfortable. Unaware. Untested. Soft.

Skip slid along the dock, hands tucked in the sleeves of his too-big coat, his expression casual as summer.

"Any luck?" he called with a grin, voice just shy of mocking.

One of the boys shrugged. "Just eels."

"Better than crabs." Skip shot back, pulling a face that earned a chuckle.

Edgar grinned despite himself. "You fish, then?"

"Oh no. I talk to fish. They tell me stories. I just pretend to catch them."

The other boys laughed, and within seconds, Skip was one of them — lounging like a stray dog in their midst, spinning tales of a sailor who lost his hand to a dogfish, or the man who netted a harbor seal and claimed it was a mermaid.

"Too easy," Skip grinned to himself, fingers brushing the handle of a small folding knife tucked into his coat — picked earlier that morning from the pocket of a loud man too drunk to notice.

Edgar turned just as Skip tucked the blade deeper into his pocket. "Have you ever ridden a horse?"

The grin on Skip's face grew wider.

— *Chapter 6* —

The harbor was still visible behind them, but Beth's pace had quickened. Martha tugged gently on Moses' lead, glancing back one last time. A breath of salt wind carried the sound of gulls and cart wheels. Dock Street had grown quieter, though the tension inflicted by Lord Morgrave lingered like a foul presence.

As they turned onto the upper road, the Inn's stone wall came into view, and with it, a row of white linens swaying from a crooked clothesline. Two Irish maids knelt by a steaming basin, scrubbing bed sheets with raw—lye burnt hands.

"Hello, Miss Beth!" Lacey called.

"You come for laundry or just the gossip?" her sister Betsy asked in jest.

Beth smiled faintly. "Neither today, my friends. Just passing through after a long day." She slowed to chat with them, welcoming a moment with like-minded women.

Martha guided the cart to a halt with Moses the goat pulling while Argon fixed his gaze on a chattering squirrel. Her eyes caught a sudden flash of gold at Lacey's throat— a little cross that swung and glimmered as the maid laughed. The brightness stirred a fond memory of Pashanok's own locket, heavy gold shining against his chest where he kept it hanging from a tough leather thong. For a breath, she felt his hand on her shoulder, leaving her with a smile in her heart.

"What of that new ship arrived in the harbor, Beth?" Betsy inquired.

"Yes, Beth. We clamored to the walk for a look-see," Lacey pointed at the railed rooftop platform atop the Inn. "The *Deliverance*. A three-masted brig flying the Union Jack, she is."

"Just another merchant on route to New Amsterdam, looking to top off her hold for trade," Beth filled in.

"We have a few passengers aboard the Inn here. A family of English—parents, daughter, and son," Betsy ran the roster. "A Lord, he says, and a few others we haven't seen yet."

"He's no Lord if you ask me," Lacey shot her sister a look and nodded. "A real right scoundrel made up as one, he is."

Martha couldn't help herself. "Acts tall, red hair. Carries a riding crop?"

"That's the one, missy," Lacey whispered. "Innkeeper said he's been here before, years ago."

"Back when he had all his fingers," Betsy laughed.

As if on cue, a loud voice could be heard barking orders at a chambermaid on the top floor. "Do not touch that case, you stupid sow! Leave me at once!"

Both women stiffened. Lacey muttered something in Gaelic.

"He's already here," Betsy whispered again, eyes wide. "Why do you think we're outside?"

Beth's expression darkened. "Be careful, ladies. Don't give him opportunity to catch you alone."

"We never are," Lacey replied.

"God be with us," Betsy said as they crossed themselves in unison. They scurried back to their work, heads down; Beth and Martha turned down the lane toward home.

Martha touched Auntie Beth's sleeve later as they continued on, "Did you know that man was here before? Why does his voice make you jump so?"

Beth hesitated. She weighed her words carefully, then explained with parental concern, "Because I've heard of what he does, that Lord Morgrave. A man like that isn't just a hunter of debt and runaways. There are horrific stories—of girls taken from their homes and sold across the sea. Disappeared forever, but no one knows for sure."

"That sly grin on his face . . . when he looked at me."

Beth stopped her. "When did he look at you?"

Beth's intense concern flickered.

"I mean," she calmed herself and asked, "How did he notice you in the crowd?"

Martha understood her mentor's protective love. She closed her eyes and pictured the scene as if she were living it for the second time, except now her emotions poured out in a kind of visionary code.

"The spirit of the harbor was jumping … with teeth like … blood in the water … and I was searching for a shark … and when I found it—I mean him … I tried to look away, but I was … caught in … gray eyes. I felt awful for you, Auntie, because I drew attention to us."

She wiped a tear from her eye.

"And he started to—and then Reverend Mayhew …"

Auntie Beth gave her a hug, held her shoulders and looked her in the eye. "You are a natural girl, Martha. You feel the spirit of things in your soul, and you should always listen to that. You are deeply bound to **Keesoq** in a beautiful way . . . in a way that protected us today. You didn't know Reverend Mayhew would be there, but Keesoq did. These things happen as they will."

Martha hugged her in response, cherishing the loving contact.

Argon nuzzled her hand and leaned against her leg.

"Who is Keesoq really, Auntie?" she asked after they resumed walking.

Beth stared wistfully to the path ahead, "Well . . . you're lucky, dear. Pashanok can explain that far better than I could."

A faint breeze lifted the edge of Martha's sleeve, carrying with it the scent of sea salt and clay. For a moment she thought she heard something deep and low beneath the rustle of the pines — not words exactly, but a breath, as if the island itself were listening. It passed as quickly as it came, leaving her strangely comforted. Argon's ears twitched. He heard it too.

They walked on in silence for some time, the sound of wheels and hooves softening under a canopy of leaves. The farther they got from the village, the more Martha noticed how the natural spirit of the island returned; filled in with voices all its own. "I am a natural girl," she thought. "I feel it deep in my bones."

Noepe agreed. Grasshoppers buzzed. Crickets chirped. A heron lifted from the creek, its wings beating a few times before catching the breeze. Martha let her shoulders relax. She noticed the stains on her dress that Charlie created with his tears, and her frown turned to a smile. "Life leaves a mark no matter what," she mused. "If that doesn't come out, I'll stitch a little bunny there."

"This girl." Beth mused to herself as well. "I wish I had half her wisdom at that age."

The island sounds of Noepe retreated, signaling a new human presence. A low murmuring melody wafted through the trees. Then came a shout. A sharp whistle. The field master up ahead.

A line of enslaved laborers, mostly women and children, trudged up from the corn rows. They were moving in the opposite direction towards Beth and Martha, their backs bent from heat and toil. A man with a hefty cane barked orders, waving it forward along the lane.

Among the group, Daisy lingered toward the rear, just enough for them to notice. Her dress was damp with sweat, her hands raw. She slowed but dared not stop.

"Hi," Martha whispered, falling into step.

Daisy glanced at the master, then back. "Ssssh Martha. Please . . . You don't talk to me."

"I brought something," Martha said, reaching into her basket and pulling out a handful of wild raspberries wrapped in a little stained cloth.

Daisy's eyes widened. "I can't," she said quickly. "They'll say I stole it."

"But, it's a gift."

"It doesn't matter." Daisy looked away. "We don't even own the rags we wear—everything belongs to them, like us."

The shock of realization stunned Martha, and before

she could reply, Daisy shuffled off, melting into the line as the field master glared at Martha and put his hand on the coiled whip at his side.

"Martha!" Beth exclaimed.

The field master gave a start toward them and Martha didn't move. Argon bared his teeth with a low growl as the fur on his back stood high.

"That dog gets loose and I'll have his hide for my hearth!" The tyrant exclaimed with clenched teeth.

Martha raised both of her hands, "He has his own mind!"

"Hear that Flanagan?" A man following laughed derisively, "The little wretch is challenging you!"

"C'mon honey," Beth implored, and then whispered in her ear, "Leave this for later, dear. Trust me."

"Get on with ya!" shouted the young man bringing up the rear. "Het! Het! Het!" He drove the poor workers like cattle.

For some time, Beth's face was hard, teeth clenched. Martha saw her anger and honestly asked from the heart, "How can they do this to children? I even recognized a few from the orphanage, like Daisy!" Her hands balled into fists.

Beth waited a long time before speaking. The line of workers had passed some distance. "Sometimes, my dear girl, the world is too wicked to explain. This too shall pass when good people stand up."

"Why can't I give Daisy some berries?" Martha asked.

"There was a girl once, before you were born," she said quietly. "She found a pearl in a bay oyster. Small, but beautiful. She kept it hidden where she slept. A slave master found her out and beat her half to death as a warning to the rest."

Martha felt sick.

"Before Caroline created the orphanage, he threw her on the steps of the church and left her there. Caroline tended to her for months. But she never truly recovered."

"Did she die?"

"Too soon." Beth nodded. "And that's when Caroline decided to create the orphanage."

"So . . . a good thing happened for all the other children. I mean . . . that girl. It's almost like . . . she was the pearl in a way?"

"A pearl of inspiration for Caroline, she was." Beth looked to the heavens in realization.

"This girl." She said to herself. "Heaven help her."

They walked the rest of the way in silence, until the trees broke open to a soft glade filled with wildflowers. Above them, gulls spiraled over the cliffs of Great Harbor. Smoke curled into the sky—thin and silver. A low hum of tribal song drifted on the late afternoon breeze.

"Are they at **Katama** already?" Martha asked.

Beth nodded. "Noepe summons them by the moon."

— Chapter 7 —

From the ridge, the land opened like a great green fan toward the sea. The dunes rolled away to the south, their crests crowned with beach grass and scrub oak, until they met the pale sweep of Katama's outer beach. Beyond, the Atlantic stretched unbroken, the white comb of the surf flashing in the late afternoon sun.

The Wampanoag summer camp lay perched high on the Katama ridgeline—a temporary village of dome shaped **wetu**, cooking **pohtap**, drying racks strung with namohs, and the great **wôpanâakôk** enjoying the balmy summer **eškwete·wi.**. Children darted between the dwellings, their laughter mingling with the thump of a drum somewhere at the camp's center. Women worked at bead-work and weaving, their hands quick, voices carrying in song over the warm air.

A line of canoes rested on the sand below, their hulls drawn high above the tide line. From here, the camp looked timeless, as if the sea and the wind had shaped it the same way for ten-thousand summers. The path bent gently toward the cliffs, where the summer sun dipped low behind the pines.

As Beth and Martha approached, two boys sprang up from a game of stones at the edge of the camp. One was tall and quick, wore a necklace of carved shell beads and shark's teeth. He playfully elbowed at his younger brother before hitching his thumb toward them.

"Tobiasquash!" Martha called.

Her cousin teased with his mock snarl. "Little wusqôhs! You again Môsi?" He turned to his friend and mimicked a scared rabbit, adding a squeal.

The other boy flashed his teeth and growled like a **cheecheemoo.**

Martha feigned surprise and they laughed.

Beth continued on ahead, carrying a gift for Pashanok's family.

Tobiasquash gestured to his friend who strode forward to take Moses' reins and tied him to a sapling. The goat bleated a few times as he started in on the fresh leaves of a little bush.

"Moses will be happy here." Martha said.

"What word did you say for the goat, Môsi?" Tobiasquash laughed, "Moses? Môsi? What is a Moses? Is it a Môsi too? No?"

"A name, Tobi . . . not a what." She shook her head and smiled, "He leads us, or so he thinks he does . . . stubborn goat."

Tobiasquash snorted and corrected her with a gleam of pride, "In my family's words, he is what he does. **nuppanashômut** — the one who finds the path. But names are not for goats, or dogs, or animals. They are who they are. To them. Like you are. To you. Môsi."

Martha looked at him quizzically, shrugged and shook her head, then walked past him toward the camp. She understood the idea of what he said, but not the why.

Why were native things always unspoken when words seemed so much easier to her? Tobiasquash said the spirits were shy and talking just frightened them away. This made more sense to her in the wild where human voices stood out like a foghorn in the mist. But in people places? Like the village or home?

Martha smiled faintly at Tobiasquash's tone, but her mind had already wandered to the people she'd passed in town that morning—the way some of the villagers glanced aside, and how some in the tribe did the same. They thought themselves different from one another in every way that mattered. But the looks were the same. The whispers were the same.

In the end, both feared what didn't fit neatly into their world. And to them, she and Auntie Beth were exactly that.

As if to read her mind, Tobiasquash said, "We don't have your villages of dead wood boxes to live in. We live in all places and all places live in us."

"But . . . " She went to argue and found no words.

A group of young children gleefully ran up to Martha with their aunts and mothers watching from a distance, each carrying a welcome gift of some sort. A few had little shells while others had animals woven from grass or an especially beautiful stone. Martha had no place for it all, so it became a grand game of "show and tell", with Martha joining them mimicking animal and bird sounds. Their carefree dancing and beautifully tanned bodies felt as much a part of the place as the wind and grass, the older ones with deerskin wrapped about their waists while the little ones played without the burden of covering. Behind her, one boy kept touching her curly long hair with deep curiosity while holding his own in comparison. She turned at the tugging and he ran away, embarrassed. The girls giggled and reached out to stroke it too.

A little girl took Martha by the hand and led her into the camp over to a group of women who were using sharp **poohquahaug** shells to prepare **namohs** for drying. She nodded to them and took her seat on a grass mat within the circle next to an older girl who gave her a stone and pointed at the basket with fish in it. Martha truly appreciated being included, despite her differences in appearance to them. Another girl put a **ahtuck nôp** across her lap with a small **wuskëtom** board and showed her how to cut and clean the fish for drying. She watched another scrape the detritus into the paws of a waiting raccoon. An older woman seated next to Martha clicked her tongue as she ran Martha's embroidered dress between her fingers. She raised her eyebrows and the other women chuckled. Martha surprised them by purring exactly like a cat, and they all laughed.

The camp was divided into family clans, each with their own dome-shaped wetu fashioned from large bent branches and covered with woven grass mats, a constantly smoldering **pohtap**, and racks for drying meat in the sun. The spaces within the camp weren't strictly delineated, so people walked casually from group to group, joining in games, tasting each others cooking or just spending time in each others company. In one way or another they were all family anyway, with the typical similarities and differences all people have. At the close of each day as the sunlight drew down the tribe would build a large pohtap at the center of the camp just to watch the flames and the sparks shoot up into the heavens, sing songs and tell stories of their day. Fire had a freedom and power they respected, a life of its own that communed with the spirit of the sky. Sometimes the sky reached down with fire of its own followed by the angry echoing crash of thunder. There were no mysteries to this life, just the spirit of things as they've always existed.

Beth watched Martha naturally fall right into step with the tribal flow, their customs and language. She was "Môsi" to them, a Wampanoag translation of "Martha" that meant "beloved daughter of two peoples." Beth however, being a full European followed more cautiously, her eyes moving over the camp and its clans with quiet respect. Strange as it would seem, she worried less about her pock scarred countenance than she did about her ties to the villagers. Assumptions had been made by both communities on the island, and the Wampanoags welcomed her more honestly than her own people did. Just then, Pashanok emerged from the shadows, his tall frame lean but strong, his hair tied back with a twist of leather.

He extended a hand and gave a welcome nod to Beth with a smile. She bowed her head with a smile in response, Her European words "Thank you." immediately sounded out of place without meaning to. She bowed her head again and shrugged bashfully.

Pashanok laughed. He pulled her close with a hug and led her along to his family near the edge of the cliff. His native wife **Nunaquas** rose from the group of women and accepted Beth's gift of flowers and incense. She was a beautiful woman whose athletic stature stood out among the others, always with a smile and warm eyes for those she loved. Her children had Pashanok's fierce determination, a trait that Môsi also inherited. Nunaquas held Beth's hand to her cheek, then did the same with Pashanok's hand. Their children ran up and wrapped their arms around his legs.

Beth was slowly growing accustomed to the tribal custom in which children belonged to the women's family lines rather than to any single man. Pashanok gave it no heed one way or another. To him, the raising of children by strong women was a matter of tribal continuity, and had little to do with the love he shared with her or the pride he felt for Môsi. Once a family was established, loyalties were rarely challenged.

The Reverend despised the custom and judged the entire tribe with biblical fire and brimstone for it, yet he also said, "If not for their native ways, what purpose would I have here? I was not sent to save the chosen, was I?"

The words rang in her ears as she knelt to accept a small shell gift from one of Môsi's half-sisters.

That night, the camp settled in around the bright glowing coals of the simmering fire. The senior clan **keesoqâw, Wampanui**t, took his seat on a log polished with years of use and motioned for Môsi and the other children to come closer. They all settled down on mats of woven grass. Even Tobiasquash sat still, admonishing his friends to show respect.

"This is the history of how Aquinnah was formed." Wampanuit began in a low, strong voice. He raised his right hand high above his head and made the perfect screech of an eagle. While the young ones watched the hand above, the adults saw him toss a small stone into the fire with the other that created a dramatic burst of sparks. He was a master story teller doing his finest work.

"A curious **squaëses** asked me the other day." He singled out Môsi with a gesture, "How did the Aquinnah cliffs come to be red like they are?"

The group turned to Môsi, and she self-consciously nodded.

Wampanuit let the moment breathe, his gaze sweeping over the children until even the smallest sat still. He leaned forward slightly, his voice dropping to a slow, deep rhythm.

"Long ago… when all people were one tribe," he began, "and the shores of Noepe were crowded with many, many feet. There were giants then… and there were the little people too. A grand multitude of creatures — some who lived in the water, some who flew in the air, and some who walked as we do."

His arms opened wide, hands turning to shape the invisible crowd. "Among them was the greatest of our kin — **Moshup,** the giant. His head brushed the clouds when he stood, and when he walked, the ground trembled like the beat of many drums."

Wampanuit rose to his full height and took a long,

deliberate step sideways, the children giggling as the dust puffed up under his heel. "He could step from island to island as he pleased," he said, lifting one great foot and setting it down again, "and in the deep waters between, he caught the huge **pôhtam** with his bare hands."

With a sudden sweeping motion, Wampanuit bent low, plunging one arm as if into the depths, his face tightening with effort. He hauled his arm upward in a great arc, shaking it so the imaginary water flew in glittering drops from his fingers. "Up, up came the whale, thrashing and bellowing!"

The children gasped, their eyes wide. Môsi's breath caught; she found herself mimicking his motion, feeling the cold rush of the ocean along her skin, the heavy tail flailing against her grasp.

"Moshup cared for the people of Noepe," Wampanuit continued, his tone now warm and full. "In the long winters, when sickness and hunger walked in every dwelling, when the winds cut through fur and skin alike— Moshup would feed us. He dragged his great catch up the high cliffs of Aquinnah. The whales were so many that their blood spilled down into the clay, painting it red as the sun at day's end."

He paused here, letting the children see it—the crimson streams down the face of the cliffs, the smell of salt and iron in the air.

"But," he said at last, and his voice dropped low, "when the people grew greedy, they stopped casting their nets. They stopped hunting the seas. They waited for

Moshup to feed them, though their hands were strong and the waters full. Their hearts grew small. So… he left."

Wampanuit straightened, his shadow stretching across the firelight. "He turned his great back on Noepe and trudged away—far away—to the land of giants. And there he remains, sleeping among his own people. Only the cliffs remember his gift to us, their red faces telling all who look upon them—"

He let his gaze travel slowly around the circle, the firelight catching in his eyes. "—Moshup was here."

"When the wind is from the west, listen well—for it may carry the footstep of Moshup, returning to see if our hearts have grown."

Tobiasquash began a chant, soon followed by the children who all joined in together—

Kishkuwôk nashau, Moshup!
(KISH-koo-wock NAH-shah, MOE-shup!)
Peequtamun-nôeese!
(pee-koo-TAH-mun nuh-WEE-suh)

West wind, Moshup
Look upon our hearts!

Later, Martha sat beside Beth near the dying embers. They heard Argon who yipped a few times in his sleep. The night was settling in quietly. In the distance, waves lapped the dark shore. A **mukquosh** hooted from the crevasse of an old tree nearby.

They heard footsteps approaching from the cliffs. Pashanok appeared at the edge of the glowing firelight. "Everyone is settled now, off to the land of dream spirits." he mused. "Will you stay Beth? You and Martha are welcome to rest with my clan."

Beth stood and met Pashanok with a hug and a kiss, "We still have much to do starting early in the morning. Martha has chores and . . ." she trailed off.

"You waste no time with pleasantries," he teased.

"Oh Pasha." Beth ran her fingers through his hair. "You could return to the cottage with us."

Martha fiddled self-consciously with a stick in the fire, adjusting the coals to bring up a flame.

"I think that would be wise." Pashanok said, his expression sharpening. He started towards the goat cart and Argon. "After what happened in town today with that pirate Morgrave, I want to know you'll be okay tonight." The sun had set but there was still an hour of twilight and the moon was full for another day or two.

Beth's heart skipped a beat, from a combination of love, excitement and apprehension. "But . . . how . . . " She and Martha followed him. ". . . did you know about Morgrave?"

"You know who you're talking to, right?" Pashanok turned to them and grinned.

As they approached the cottage, Martha's skin felt hot and shivery at the same time. She felt Argon tense up. The goat shuffled over to it's pen, pulling the cart along. Pashanok felt the same trepidation. Something wasn't right. Beth was preoccupied with the night and relaxed her guard with Pashanok in charge. He created the relief she so anxiously dreamed of but could never fully possess.

"You stay here Beth." Pashanok broke the silence and brought her into the moment.

"Why Pasha? What . . ." He put his finger to her lips.

"Môsi. Go settle Moses into his enclosure and put up the food for the hens. I won't leave until you're back and in bed."

Martha did as she was told, confident in Pashanok's leadership.

The cottage door was slightly ajar; the curtain was pushed aside. Without a candle for light they'd never know all that happened while they were away . . . and getting that started would take some time. Pashanok slipped his hunting dagger from the sheath on his leg and opened the door in one swift motion. He slashed left and right then stood at the ready, listening. Nothing. He checked the bedroom. Nothing. No ambush. No sign of damage.

"Could the wind have blown this open?" Pashanok pointed to the open door as he beckoned to Beth, nervously waiting outside.

She passed by him and looked around, turning back, she said, "It may have, but I'm sure we closed it . . . although we were busy with all of my wares. I just don't know."

Martha came around the corner, the look of concern melted when she saw Pashanok with his knife. She ran to him and gave him a long, tight hug.

"Whoa. Whoa there." He held the knife above his head. "I'll sheathe this blade, then you shall have your embrace."

She giggled, stood back, then resumed her loving assault with extra enthusiasm after he sheathed the knife. Beth joined in and for a moment she had the little family in her cottage that she'd always dreamed of. For a moment she was not scarred, not judged, only loved.

After getting a candle lit with the back of his blade and a flint on tinder, Pashanok eventually left.

As Martha got ready for bed, she couldn't get the sweet floral scent of the beach rose out of her mind. "Do you smell that, Beth?"

"You mean the candle, dear?" she responded.

"No Auntie . . . a flower. A sweet smell."

Martha didn't push the matter. There on her pillow lay the fresh pink blossom of a beach rose, its petals salt-soft and familiar. She remembered the prickle of its thorn on her walk into the village, and knew at once who might have left it. Only one person could have done that . . . Edgar. But he wouldn't dare, would he?

— *Chapter 8* —

Skip hopped down from the gangway, the boards creaking under his light step. The morning air on Dock Street was already busy with wagon wheels and gull cries. Morgrave stood just beyond the wharf, his gloved hands resting on his walking stick.

"Well?" Morgrave's voice was smooth, almost disinterested.

"Captain says we'll be taking on fresh supplies before the tide turns tomorrow night," Skip replied, eyes darting up the street. "Means we've got a bit of shore time… if we make the most of it."

Morgrave's gaze narrowed. "And you will."

Skip grinned, tipping his cap before slipping into the crowd.

Halfway up Water Street toward the inn, he spotted Edgar outside his family's barn, working a currycomb through the bay gelding's mane. Edgar looked up, his usual guarded expression softening with curiosity.

"Going for a ride?" Skip asked, leaning on the fence.

"Maybe."

"Good," Skip said. "I've got something to show you —out by the old cottage near the lane." He let the words hang, as if the destination itself were a secret worth chasing.

Edgar hesitated, glancing toward the house. "I'd have to ask my—"

But Skip had already swung the barn door open, stepping inside as though invited. "Won't take long," he said, running a hand along the horse's flank. "You want to sit here brushing all day, or do you want to see something worth talking about?"

From the porch of the house, Edgar's father appeared, a ledger tucked under one arm. "Off somewhere, Edgar?"

"Just a short ride," Edgar answered, his voice steady but not quite confident.

His father's eyes moved from Edgar to Skip, then back again. "Mind you're back before the bell."

Skip was already leading the horse out, his grin flickering just long enough for Edgar to notice—and to wonder exactly what he'd agreed to, not realizing Skip followed him the night before.

The sun rose soft and golden over the forest, brushing the cottage trim with light. Inside, the air was still, yet something felt unsettled. Hoof prints near the garden gate. A crushed fern by the path. A faint scuff on the wooden threshold. Beth noticed each detail without speaking of it—her thoughts drifting uneasily toward who might have come during the night. A dream? A memory? Or a very real intruder?

Martha, already awake, folded the edge of her blanket over the small pink blossom resting on her pillow, tucking it out of sight. She couldn't bear to throw it away. Nor could she endure Auntie Beth's disappointment if she knew where it came from. The scent still clung to the linens—a wild, salty sweetness that didn't belong indoors.

They dressed and began their morning quietly, moving through familiar motions with the restraint of people carrying unspoken thoughts. Beth prepared bread warmed on a cast iron pan and served it with soft goat's milk butter and a spoonful of her best blackberry preserve. They drank warm tea with a hint of dried mint and honey, seated across from each other at the small table, but their eyes didn't meet often.

Then—hoof-beats.

Distant at first, then unmistakable.

Beth froze. Her hand drifted towards a knife beside the stove. Martha slipped from her stool and pressed her back to the wall near the pantry.

The sounds drew closer, and a voice rang out: "Martha! You in there?" A pause, then a different voice— laughter, brash and sharp-edged. "We come bearing flowers!"

Beth moved to the door and yanked it open with the full authority of her stature. Her presence filled the doorway like a thundercloud.

Two boys sat bareback on a bay horse in the path beyond the gate. Edgar held the reins, his cheeks flushed with nervous excitement. The other boy sat behind him, his arm slung lazily around Edgar's waist, grinning with the smug ease of a troublemaker who knew he'd stirred something up.

Martha peered out from behind the curtains, hoping to remain hidden. Edgar's eyes lit up when he saw her.

"Did you get the beach rose I left you?" he called.

Martha's face went pale. She shook her head quickly, hoping to protect him.

"But—but I left it on your pillow," he said with confusion, blinking. "This morning. I mean—last night. I—"

Beth turned slowly toward her. Her brow lifted. Her gaze sharpened. Then she turned back to Edgar, now stone-faced.

"You entered our home," she said. "You broke in. You are not welcome here, Edgar. Not again. Not ever. I will be speaking to your father about this!"

The other boy, still chuckling, leaned forward and whispered something in Edgar's ear, clearly pleased with himself.

"Leave now. And do not speak to Martha again."

Beth's voice held no hint of negotiation.

The air grew suddenly still. Edgar opened his mouth to object, but the boy behind him gave the horse a sharp slap on the flank. With a startled whinny, the animal bolted down the path, sweeping Edgar—and all his confused affection—away in a cloud of dust.

Martha's heart fell as she watched him go.

Then she turned and ran to her bed.

And cried.

Edgar was crying too as he clung to the horse's mane, blinking back tears and trying to keep his posture straight while Skip, seated behind him, cackled with satisfaction.

Edgar said nothing. His jaw tightened. A lump

formed in his throat.

They turned the corner at speed—too fast—and collided directly with Pashanok, who had been tracking hoofprints along the forest path. It was chaos. The horse reared and bolted, all three figures thrown in different directions. Pashanok tumbled hard into the brush, the boys onto the dirt road.

Pashanok had heard them coming. He had planned to intercept and question them. But now, bruised and blinking in the brambles, he sat up and began checking himself for injuries. In a rage, he stood and lunged at the whimpering boy across the path, yanked him roughly to his feet.

Edgar, still stunned, emplored, "I'm so sorry! Sir! Are you—"

"Pashanok bent down, pulling him close, face to face. Edgar saw the fire blazing in his eyes. "**CHEECHEEMOO**!" he roared, the word cracking the air like a whip. "You bring shame upon your clan!" His voice jumped between Wampanoag and English. "That horse is sacred life, a gift of Keesoq—not a plaything for your foolishness!"

The language blurred, but the meaning was crystal clear.

"Where is the other boy?" Pashanok shook Edgar, then shoved the petrified boy to the ground. He turned in a circle while scanning the forest around them.

Skip, trembling behind a tree, had gone silent. His breath came quick and shallow, and his heartbeat thudded like a drum. Then something caught his eye—a bright metallic glint in the leaves, there, by his foot. Something golden.

His fear paused for one precious second as his attention focused on the small locket lying among the forest debris. With the practiced experience of a seasoned thief, he carefully snatched it and slipped it into his pocket.

Then came the pounce. With catlike speed, Pashanok leapt into the brush and dragged Skip out by the arm.

"HELP! HELP ME!" Skip shrieked. "SAVAGE! DON'T EAT ME!"

Pashanok grit his teeth. The boy wriggled free for a moment, bowled over Edgar and ran off like a frightened ahtuck, bounding through the forest towards town. Edgar took the opportunity to make an escape himself, although he felt terribly guilty and wished he'd never met his new "friend" Skip.

Pashanok was still a bit dazed. Then came the ache. Not just in his ribs or twisted ankle, but something older, deeper in his heart.

His fingers reached for the space beneath his collarbone, where the locket had always rested . . . the one with Elizabeth's miniature portrait painted inside. *GONE!*

Pashanok knelt where the boy had hidden, searching the brush again, turning over every leaf and stone, combing the forest floor for a glint of gold. He pressed his hand to the dirt, breathing in the scent of crushed pine and earth. *It should have been there.*

A stillness grew in him. And from that stillness, a voice rose — quiet, but clear:

This is the cost of betraying your people to befriend the **nanapashômutash**. You bend your soul for them, and what do you reap? Heartbreak. Go back to your

Wampanoag family. Live a real life.

He shut his eyes and clenched his fist. Not now. Not yet. Pashanok retreated to the peace of the forest where he could think, his mind consumed with the lost locket and how it might change his life.

Beth had watched the boys gallop away down the path, hair in the wind and barely under control. She closed the cottage door and pushed the them out of her mind. The peace of her sacred privacy had been broken for the first time. Neighbors were expected to stop by unannounced, but this? It was a crime, even if committed by stupid boys. She stood in the great room, staring down the path, pondering her and Martha's security with growing determination. It was no good, she thought— their world had been tainted with a stain no one could remove.

She found Martha huddled on her bed, knees drawn tight, shoulders trembling. "Oh, my little dove," Beth murmured, crossing the room without hurry. She sat beside her, letting the mattress dip until their weight balanced. Her hand moved in slow, steady circles over Martha's back. "This is just another day. You'll learn — it's not the end of the world." She said to Martha and . . . to herself.

"But it feels like the end of *my world*!" Martha's voice broke, the words tumbling out with her sobs. Beth felt the honesty cut deep, but for different reasons. She sighed heavily, fingering the edge of Martha's blanket.

Beth drew her in, holding her until she could feel the

girl's breathing begin to slow.

After a long pause, Martha's voice came again, quieter.

"Why do those people from the ship whisper when I walk by? They don't know me. Edgar doesn't, but—he didn't stop them either. And some of the tribal girls do it too—it's like I'm cursed somehowl. Why?"

Beth rested her cheek lightly against Martha's hair.

"People whisper for all kinds of reasons, my sweet dove.   Sometimes because they don't understand. Sometimes because they do, and they're afraid to show it."

"That makes no sense."

"No, it doesn't" Beth agreed. "Most people, no matter where they come from, village or tribe, notice what's different before they notice what's the same. It's easier for them than looking closer."

Martha frowned into Beth's shoulder. "So I'll always be different."

Beth leaned back just enough to see her face. "Different isn't bad. But it does mean you'll have to choose, again and again, how to carry yourself outside these walls. Do you let others decide who you are, or do you decide for yourself?"

Martha didn't answer, but she didn't look away either.

"Trust your spirit." Beth kissed her forehead, "Guide your heart by the truth you know. Protect all that you love."

Outside, a flock of crows flew noisily overhead, their dark shadows cascading across the garden. Inside, the faint scent of a beach rose lingered between them, soft and steady, like a reminder that storms pass, and flowers return.

— *Chapter 9* —

Pashanok lay still as stone in the underbrush, one knee pressed to the earth, his breath slow and measured. The forest wrapped around him like a cloak—thick with fern, root, and shadow. Every leaf above caught the light like glass; every movement ahead was a ripple through a sacred pool.

Just beyond the tangle of thorn and vine, two figures blundered noisily: Lord Goodwin Morgrave in his dark riding coat, and Skip the cabin boy, lean and jittery as a squirrel. They pushed aside branches and kicked through brittle stems, searching—though not for food or firewood, but treasure.

The boy carelessly swung a glinting object on a leather thong, letting it loop and coil around his finger like a toy charm or trinket.

Elizabeth's locket.

With one careless flick, it slipped free and flew into the leaves near Sharp's boot. He gasped and moved to find it again.

A sharp crack rang out—a backhanded slap that twisted Skip's head sideways.

"Give that to me, you stupid worthless little worm."

Skip went rigid, stunned. Then quickly stooped,

retrieving the locket with trembling fingers. He held it out in both hands like a wounded little bird.

"Y-yes sir. I have it here, m'Lord."

Moregrave snatched it without looking and dropped it into a leather pouch that hung from his belt, pressing the flap closed with a click of brass.

Pashanok narrowed his eyes.

The scent of wickedness was strong here. He shifted his weight slightly—silent as wind threading through pine.

Then came a change. Lord Morgrave's voice softened, syrupy and coiled.

"Tell Uncle Goodwin, my boy… my sweet little Skipper," he crooned. "What happened here this morning? Something about a rich boy, a runaway horse, and some… ssssavage?"

Skip gave a snort of laughter, then launched into his retelling—Edgar's ridiculous flower offering, the burst of jealousy, Martha's temper, the mess of limbs and barking and bruises. Morgrave smiled with slow pleasure as if sipping some private tea.

Pashanok could not catch the words—but the laughter, the mocking tone, the word savage—he heard them all.

He crept closer. One step. Then another. Bare feet pressing softly into moss and soil.

"Did either of them see your find?" Morgrave asked, looking for more.

"No sir. Not a glance. It was in my pocket before either one knew it existed," Skip said proudly, puffing up like a rooster.

"Then it couldn't have belonged to them," Sharp

muttered. "A little treasure like this… they'd have torn their hair out if they lost it."

Pashanok could bear it no longer, now that he'd seen the locket. He rose from the brush like a wave rising from still water, sudden and fierce.

"That is MINE!" he thundered, voice cutting through the trees like a blade. "Give it to me—NOW."

Skip shrieked and stumbled backward, nearly falling into a patch of thorns. "That's HIM! It's—it's—it's the—SAVAGE!"

He ducked behind his "Uncle Goodwin", shivering and small.

The older man did not flinch. One hand rose in a gentle gesture, palm out, as if calming a horse. The other slid to his belt.

Pashanok saw it—but he was too late.

The dagger flashed before he could fully dodge it. Steel kissed skin.

A red line split open across his forearm like bark peeled from a birch. The sting came hot and fast.

Pashanok leapt back, teeth clenched, weight shifted low—ready to counter, but Morgrave pressed forward, blade slashing through the air.

This time he was too late.

Pashanok was gone—already swallowed by the trees. The only sound left was the breath of branches brushing each other in the hush.

Lord Morgrave stood in the clearing, dagger raised, his chest rising. A moment passed. Then another. The edge of the world seemed to hold its breath.

At last, Morgrave wiped the blade and slid it back

into its sheath with the cool precision of a butcher.

"Said it was his, did he?" he muttered. "That wild dog, that forest-stained mongrel. He thought it belonged to him?"

He turned to Skip.

"You're sure he didn't see you pocket it?"

"I swear it on my mum's grave, sir."

"Well," Morgrave said, brushing pine needles from his coat, "your mum's grave not withstanding... he must've guessed. Or lied. Either way, this locket is far too fine for the likes of him."

He tapped the pouch at his side, then a thought came to him.

"No, this belonged to someone else. A rich family, I'll wager. Perhaps even—"

He pulled the locket out and pried it open for the first time. There inside, glowing with all her youth and beauty was the unblemished image of Elizabeth.

Morgrave stared into the distance, his look inscrutable.

"Ahhh." He paused and spoke with quiet venom, "I recognize this face from many years ago. Blue eyes. That auburn hair. A haughty little spine. Wouldn't be the first merchant's daughter to run wild. The question is, how did this locket get here and well, if she's still on this glorified sand bar of an island . . . that opens a number of profitable doors."

He clapped Skip on the shoulder, and the two turned toward the village, the boy still glancing over his shoulder as if the woods might spit Pashanok back out to attack him at any moment.

Under deep cover, unseen in the lattice of vines, maple and oak, Pashanok crouched again "cursed cheecheemoo"—his breath now quick and shallow. Blood slid in a thin line down his fingers, dripping to the forest floor with the metallic scent of rusted iron.

He tore a strip of bark from a nearby tree, wrapped it tightly around his forearm, and knotted it with his teeth.

He would not limp. Not now. Not ever.

He would tell Beth what he had seen—and only Beth.

Beth was working at her spinning wheel when she heard an urgent knock at the door. She swept the curtain aside to see Pashanok, his right forearm tightly bound with a strip of bark, blood dripping from his hand.

She yanked the door open and ran to the water barrel by the hearth, grabbing a clean cloth before rushing back to where he was now seated.

"Oh my God! Pasha—what happened?"

He began unwrapping the bark, but the release of pressure made the blood flow faster. He stopped, jaw tight.

"This looks deep," she said, inspecting the gash. "We need to clean and bind it properly."

He hesitated, silent for a moment. Then he looked deep into her eyes and nodded. "Yes. We must."

There was another wound he had yet to explain. The locket.

Normally, he would have gone to Wampanuit for a healing **maskutash**—remedies proven over generations. But that would invite questions. Accusations. Retaliation—

perhaps against the village. And all because he'd underestimated the strange new foreigner.

He glanced around. "Môsi isn't here?"

Beth shook her head. "No. Tobiasquash came by. I told her to go with him to the tribe, actually—to see you. She needed space after that stunt the boy pulled." She exhaled. "And she's angry with me. I banished him from contacting her again. Môsi still has so much to learn."

"I feel for our daughter, Elizabeth . . . I do. She's caught in a lifelong snare—belonging to the tribe and the village, yet claimed by neither."

At the sound of her true name, Beth flinched. "Please, Pasha... not here. Don't say my real name. It weakens your resolve. You could blurt it out without thinking somewhere and —"

She rinsed the cloth in a bowl, her hand shaking.

"I know. I know." He reached for her hand. "It just warms my heart to say it."

She pressed the cloth gently to his arm. "This," she said, nodding to his arm, "is not from a branch or a beast. Tell me what happened."

He told her everything—from the collision to the confrontation with Lord Morgrave, and about her locket.

Beth covered her mouth as he spoke. Tears welled in her eyes. "That—that evil snake. The Devil himself."

"He got the better of me, Beth. I was rash. I paid for it." He looked away. "And now he has your locket. Your portrait. It's tied to me now."

"We have to get it back. That locket belongs to us. And the tribe will notice it's missing. They'll see your wound."

He drew her into his lap, arms wrapped around her waist. Beth buried her face in his hair, her tears falling freely.

"I miss you, Pasha... I miss you every day." She pulled back just enough to look at him. "I do my work, I raise our daughter, I pretend to be someone I'm not—and it's all so fragile. Like glass. One crack and everything in our life shatters."

"These aren't normal times, Elizabeth." He rested his head on her chest. "The world changes with every new ship in the harbor. It takes courage just to exist. And yet, here we are."

She wiped her eyes and stood up. Her voice shifted—cooler now. Focused.

"Then we need a strategy. A real one. One that defeats the Devil and protects Martha."

"And what would that be?"

"Morgrave will never stop. My parents' reward is still out there—he wants to return their 'lost daughter' for a price. But it's not about honor. It's blackmail. They think I'm dead. If he brings me back, he'll extort them. And if they resist? He'll reveal that Elizabeth is wanted for theft of a Lord's property."

"So... it sounds like this Lord needs to have an accident of some kind." Pashanok smiled grimly.

"No Pasha." She paced now. "No more violence. The truth always surfaces. And the King's men would follow . . ."

"I was joking, Beth."

"This is no time for joking."

"Agreed."

"We have to put him off the scent—send him away, far and fast, chasing someone who doesn't exist."

"And how do we do that without getting so close he will see through it?"

She stopped and turned. "We talk to Reverend Mayhew. He's the only one who knows the truth about us, and Martha—he still honors Caroline's vow. Here's what I'll tell him . . . "

She laid out her plan. And as she spoke, Pashanok listened—silently proud of the woman he loved.

Martha left her 'dead wood box' home with Tobiasquash, who understood little and cared less about a girl's love interests. He knew they flew here and there like butterflies tending to flowers in the field. They were just as pretty, but you could never catch one when you wanted to. They had to land on you in their own time—or so his father always said. His cousin Môsi, he thought, had landed on poison ivy of a sort . . . and now she was paying for it with an itch in her heart.

"Break free from this unhappy place you found, Môsi. That Edgar boy has your heart in a snare, and the more you thrash about, the tighter it's going to get," he said, counseling from his hunter's mind.

She kicked a rock and stubbed her toe, hopping on one foot with a scowl.

"You don't understand anything, Tobi. You just don't."

He laughed and gave her a hip bump. "I guess you're

right. But I'm always on your side—as sure as the moon and the tides."

She bumped him back, half-smiling. "Somehow, you always make me feel better."

The path opened up into the Wampanoag summer camp, where everyone was busy with daily chores. Older boys were wrestling while others competed in spear-throwing, aiming for a straw-stuffed rabbit skin from different distances. Younger children played hunt-and-tag around the wetu of different clans. Adults went mostly unnoticed—except for a few sharp words when a fish-drying rack was knocked over or someone strayed too close to the fire.

As they approached the different clans, Tobiasquash peeled away toward a group of men gathered down near the shore where **Wuttahmin** and **Maskotae** were building a canoe alongside two older cousins. A woven basket of freshly cut eel grass lay at their feet, ready to line the fish traps. One of the men handed Tobiasquash a spear tipped with sharpened bone, its shaft worn smooth by years of use.

"Wind's in our favor today," Wuttahmin said, grinning. "We'll push the shallows and drive the namohs in tight."

Maskotae clapped Tobiasquash on the shoulder. "Mind you don't let the little ones slip past, or the women will tell us we've grown lazy."

Tobiasquash laughed, falling in with their stride as they made for the water's edge, their voices already rising to the rhythm of the work ahead.

Môsi turned toward the older girls who were

mending fishing nets. She lifted one that needed a large hole knotted back together and joined in.

The girls' conversation continued without pause.

"He is a rough one, that **Tawôtam**" said Tawasquat, a bigger girl with mature interests.

Mattaniqua laughed. "He always wants me to run when **kuhkum** insists I stay by her side."

The others giggled. Môsi laughed too.

"But you, Mar-thaa …" Tawasquat turned toward her, teasing with a sharp edge, using her English name. "You dip your paddle in the village waters, don't you?"

"You're always talking boys and paddles, Tawasquat. There are more important things to be done." Môsi lifted the net to demonstrate.

"Oh Mar-thaa, stop pretending you aren't chasing that ugly sand-head Edgar. Your foreign blood betrays us all." Tawasquat's tone hardened.

"Môsi is our **nuxkáawees**, Tawa," said **Wunnêgin** gently, placing a hand on Môsi's shoulder. "She stands for us—first and always."

Another girl agreed, "Môsi never backs down when it matters."

"No, **Sôpan**. Mar-thaa dances to their song like a slave to the **nanapashômutash**!" Tawasquat's voice rose, bitter.

Môsi glanced around. The other girls stared silently at her with a mix of curiosity and doubt. None of them had ever set foot in the village. To them, Tawasquat's accusations were spiced with intrigue.

Môsi met their eyes.

"We know there's more to this world than the

Wampanoag, Tawasquat. Even before the nanapashômutash came to Noepe, we knew of the **Nauset**, the **Mashpee**, the **Narragansett**. They are nothing more than another tribe of different people."

The younger girls had never heard those names, but Môsi's voice carried truth—and it earned their silence.

"Says the half-blood outsider," Tawasquat snapped, standing and marching away.

Mattaniqua hesitated, then followed, glancing back with a face full of confused emotion.

Sôpan slid closer. "Her **mushum** and kuhkum died from the nanapashômutash sickness," she whispered. "You can't blame her for being bitter."

"I understand all too well," Môsi said, her voice steady. "My Auntie Beth is scarred from that same sickness. It spares no one—from babies to elders. But the same can be said of our own diseases, can it not?"

The girls shivered and nodded solemnly.

"My blood is no fault of my own—no more than yours is. Isn't that true, Sôpan?" Môsi turned toward the quiet girl at the edge of the circle. "Your mushum was Mashpee. And yet you are still proud Wampanoag."

"My blood is pure," the girl said with quiet pride. "Like Tawasquat said. Yours is not, Môsi."

"Then I have the advantage, don't I?" Martha replied. "I have one foot in the village and one in the tribe. I can travel. I can speak the languages of all people. But I stand firm in one place always: Noepe."

The girls looked at each other, then back at Martha. It rang true. Deeply true.

"Don't forget this, if you ever need help with the

villagers. I am your sister. Your cousin. Your guide. Even for Tawasquat—and Wunnêgin."

Môsi caught glimpses of Tobiasquash between the heads of the girls, his laughter carrying over the wind each time his spear struck true. Now and then a flash of silver broke the water's surface, followed by the slap of a fish into the waiting basket. How different the boys were. Did they ever concern themselves with these things?

Just then, a younger boy came splashing up from the water, grinning wildly. He heaved a wet and slimy piece of kelp over Tobiasquash's shoulders and bolted toward the beach.

"You'll regret that!" Tobiasquash called, tossing his spear to Wuttahmin without missing a step.

The chase curved wide across the sand, past the drying racks, and up toward the circle of girls. Before Môsi could react, Tobiasquash barreled straight into their gathering, scattering the group in a spray of laughter and mock protest.

"You're the wusqôhs now! Run, wusqôhs! Run!" he shouted, tagging Môsi on the ankle.

The girls screamed and scattered as a mob of younger boys came barreling after them. Môsi gave Toby a glare—but a playful one—and sprinted off into the woods like a rabbit.

Tobiasquash rolled over on his back, laughing.

— *Chapter 10* —

The harbor shimmered beneath a swollen full moon, its silver light spilling across the water like a trail of molten mercury. A dozen ships and lesser craft lay at anchor, their dark hulls rocking in the gentle swell, sails furled tight against the night. The wind hummed through a forest of masts, setting the rigging to a low, constant whisper, and each turn of the tide made the dock pilings creak like old bones. The air carried a rich tangle of scents—sharp brine from the tide flats, the tarry bite of fresh pitch, and the warm, smoky drift of roasted herring from a brazier on the wharf. Now and then a gull shrieked, the sound slicing through the rhythmic slap of water against the wharf, while lantern light wavered in the windows of dockside taverns, drawing sailors and merchants like moths to a flame.

Near the docks, a row of leaning buildings hugged the wharf, their clapboard siding gray and roughened by decades of wind and salt. Among them, a low, weather-worn tavern crouched in the shadows—*The Buck and Barrel.* Its crooked eaves dripped with sea fog, and a pair of dented lanterns swung on iron brackets, casting restless light across the cobblestones. Above the door, the painted sign creaked with each gust: a stag rearing proudly over a cask, though the colors had long been bleached to ghosts by sun and spray. Laughter and the rise-and-fall of a sea shanty spilled through the warped floorboards, underscored by the clink of mugs and the occasional sharp burst of argument.

Inside, the air was thick with the mingled scents of ale, salt, and woodsmoke. The room buzzed with midsummer energy, the kind that made men linger long past their work. Candles guttered in squat pewter holders on warped tables, their flames bending in the occasional draft from the door. Tankards clanked, dice rattled across scarred tabletops, and a fiddler by the hearth scraped out a sharp, breathless tune that drove a steady tap of boots on the floorboards. Fishermen, sailors, and dock hands leaned in close over their mugs, gambling, bickering, or swapping tales of storms and sea beasts, each more outrageous than the last. Now and then, the room erupted with a burst of laughter or a shouted curse, but the rhythm of the night quickly swallowed it back into the tavern's living heartbeat.

Lord Goodwin Morgrave entered the tavern with calculated ease, his boots clean, his cloak too fine for such a place. He drew attention, but pretended not to notice. Beneath his tailored coat hung a leather pouch, and tucked within it: a locket, now resting between his fingers.

He stepped to the bar and laid a coin on the counter. "Looking for a face," he said to the barkeep, a broad-shouldered man with a broken nose and inked knuckles. "A girl who might've worked nearby a decade back. Unforgettable beauty—snow-pale skin, hair like a dusky rose."

The barkeep eyed the coin, then the locket as

Morgrave clicked it open. A miniature portrait of a beautiful young woman with curly chestnut hair and bright blue eyes gleamed in the dim light.

"Too many come and go to remember," the man muttered. "But show that around, you might stir a few memories."

Morgrave turned toward the room, holding the locket high. "Gentlemen. I seek a girl who may have once graced this island—ten years past."

A chorus of laughter came from a rowdy group of sailors.

"Who doesn't?" Shouted on exceptionally inebriated lout. "Ten years? You're that desperate, man?"

They all clanked pewter tankards and drank to their own humor.

A lean, sun-leathered sailor squinted from table nearby. "That her in the picture?" he asked.

"Indeed."

"Aye... I remember that lass. Worked by the Vincents, just up Main Street. She weren't like the others. Quiet. Didn't say much, but when she did, every man shut up to listen."

"She used to sit down by the pier," said another. "Reading. Always had a book. Some thought she was touched. Others said she came from money."

"I tried talking to her once," a third chimed in. "Got one look and forgot what I was sayin'. Never saw eyes like that."

The men chuckled, nodding with the distant reverence of sailors remembering a far-off port.

"Shame what happened," one murmured. "Thought

she died with the others in that summer plague. Never found her body, though. Just up and gone."

At the edge of the room, Skip leaned against the wall, watching. His eyes flitted from Morgrave to the men, then to a pair of drunken sailors near the door.

"You owe me for the dice throw, you fat bastard!" one shouted, slamming his mug on the table.

"You were cheating with that chipped one, I saw it!"

As voices rose, Skip nudged a stool just enough to trip one man into the other. The fight broke open like a cracked cask. Fists flew. A chair splintered. The fiddler ducked.

In the chaos, Skip slipped among the shouting crowd, hands deft as a pickpocket's prayer.

Moments later, a man by the bar reached for his coin purse—and found it gone.

"Thief!" he bellowed. "That little rat-boy took my purse!"

All eyes turned to the door, just as Skip darted into the night.

A slow silence spread across the room. The mood had soured. Morgrave closed the locket and stepped away from the bar.

"Terribly sorry for the disruption," he said with a well-practiced bow. "The boy's not mine, but he traveled with my party. Allow me to apprehend him and turn him over to the captain. Justice, after all, is still the law of the sea."

He strode out into the night after the boy, cloak flaring behind him, his voice carrying just loud enough for those in the doorway to hear.

"You won't run far, you little bastard!"

But his tone held no urgency. Only calculation.

He vanished into the shadows, chasing the illusion of discipline—while the real chase had only just begun.

Martha felt restless in bed, staring at the moonlight outside her oil cloth window, wondering how life could be so complicated in such a short period of time. She closed her eyes and drifted into a dreamy place she called middle-land, where she wasn't fully asleep or awake, just pleasantly resting. Here she could picture things of pure imagination or memories of her favorite moments, all knit together in a fantastical tapestry of dreams.

She slipped into that quiet place between waking and dreams, and found herself wandering the rows of her sacred vineyard. Moonlight pooled in silver ripples along the leaves, each grape like a bead of midnight glass. The air was sweet with the memory of crushed fruit and dyed wool drying in the sun, though no breeze stirred. Here, the world was hushed—only the faint rustle of vines and the distant whisper of the sea reached her. It felt as though the vineyard itself was alive, keeping her company, holding her safe until morning came.

Tonight, a new person appeared in the most glorious dress, like the ones she saw brides wearing at the Reverend's church. She had flowing red **wuskóonk** that fell to her waist in curls very much like her own. A small golden locket shimmered on her neck, dancing about on a thin silken thread. Her young face glowed with a soft light as if reflecting the moon, and her blue eyes sparkled like stars in the sky.

Martha was awestruck and humbled. Though her heart leaped in recognition, her mind was apprehensive. Who was this angel? Why was she here? The woman smiled ever so kindly and beckoned to her. Martha reached out and the apparition grasped her hand. Her touch was neither warm nor cold, just the same as her own hand, but the feel was like the softest baby's skin.

She followed the woman down a path where she saw animals of all kinds strolling about without a care—rabbits and foxes, a burly bear and her cubs next to grazing deer. A whippoorwill trilled from the treetops above. Everywhere, a tangle of grape vines with blossoms and the sweetest scent of beach roses. She now thought of Edgar, and shook her head a little for how foolish she felt.

The woman brought her to the center of a field high on the cliffs of Aquinnah; wildflowers danced in the moonlight. She turned to Martha and raised her palms to the sky. Island people of every kind began walking into the field from every direction. She didn't recognize any of them, but their types were clear by their attire—both young and old, tall and short, Wampanoag and European.

The woman gestured for them to stop, and they calmly halted, then started talking to each other in a low murmur. She couldn't decipher the words, but the sound was like a song. The woman reached out, held both of

Martha's hands and gazed into her eyes, touching her soul.

"You know me, child of my spirit. Even without a name, your heart remembers, Martha." Her voice the same as the others but clear like the notes of a songbird. "I am the one closest to your soul in all things, but most of all love."

The murmur of the people sounded like 'Amen' in a melodic way. Then all together they sung her name in the same way, 'Martha'. A tear formed in Martha's eye and the woman wiped it away with her delicate touch. She did know her! The stories Beth told about her! A memory burst forth in living color. A giant face coming down to kiss her forehead with red curls caressing her cheeks and the sweetest voice— that sounded—that LOOKED like this beautiful woman.

Then one of the Wampanoag men started a low drum beat that slowly increased in pace and volume, like the ticking of a clock. She remembered it from the elders' tales—the drums of war. The woman looked concerned but kept holding Martha still. She put Martha's hand to her face and it began to change... her hair slowly turned white as the drum beat faster. Martha thought to break free but was held in a trance as the woman continued to deteriorate. Her skin began scarring and one eyelid began to droop, just like . . .

The people began marching toward the cliffs. She looked away as she heard them fall, each one tumbling to the crashing waves below. All of them marching, resigned to their doom, and Martha could do nothing about it. Her heart was breaking for the sheer horror of it all.

Then the woman shed the diseased skin on her face

so that her inner brightness shone like the sun; so bright that Martha could still see her with eyes closed! She felt the love swell in her own heart, pounding in unison with her —MOTHER!

With that realization, everything started to spin. She wanted so desperately to ask thousands of questions, but the middle-land was disappearing before her eyes! With all her strength she cried out, "STOP!"—but the woman, her mother had gone.

Then, as if summoned from the shadows by her heart's command, a vast shape rose from the base of the cliffs—not monstrous, but mighty and humanlike, made of mist and moonlight. His hair streamed like kelp in the surf, his eyes dark and knowing. He looked directly at her.

"Noepe remembers you, little one," Moshup's voice resonated—not through the air—but within her chest. "You walk where my heart once walked. Do not fear what you must carry."

She reached out, but a dense fog swept between them, and the vision shattered into foam and wind. Everything obeyed. It all melted away—too soon.

Martha found herself standing barefoot in the middle of her beloved vineyard with the full moon above—a whippoorwill's mournful call swept across the fields as the tree frogs peeped and fireflies danced in the wind. She lifted the hem of her nightgown above the dew-laden grass and returned home, her heart already stirring with a restless hunger to share her questions with Auntie Beth.

— *Chapter 11* —

The full moon had just set as the first light of dawn stirred the sleepy harbor. Roosters crowed in the distance while gulls circled over fishing boats headed out to sea. An old dog barked half-heartedly from behind a garden fence. Predators and prey alike resumed their morning routines, each facing another day of survival.

Lord Goodwin Morgrave was in an unusually chipper mood as he dressed himself. His campaign boots shone brightly. His royal blue coat was brushed to perfection, and he took personal pleasure in polishing the brass buttons himself. The innkeeper had offered the service, but Morgrave declined—he trusted his own hands and no one else. As he checked for unsightly moth damage, he nodded in satisfaction. The cedar chips had done their work. Lord Morgrave examined himself in the looking glass. Today would be his day.

The people of Martin's Vineyard—as it was called by some—this unruly patch of sand overgrown with bramble and backwater folk, would learn to tremble at the sound of his name—if they didn't already.

Tipping his bi-cornered hat to a pair of early-rising gentlemen, he turned and sneered openly at the servants sweeping steps or emptying chamber pots. Lord Morgrave tapped his riding crop against his glove with rhythmic purpose, pausing only when he reached the wharf. Drake's sailors were scrubbing the decks yet again. Above them, Captain Drake sipped his morning tea at the rail with a taint of rum to start the day.

"Fine morning, good Captain!" Morgrave hailed from the dock. Drake sighed. Only one reason that black-hearted knave would sound cheerful—some poor soul is about to suffer.

"Good day, m'Lord. A cup of tea, perhaps?" He responded.

"No time for that, you lazy sod," Morgrave laughed heartily at his own insult. "We've got the Crown's business to attend to!"

Damn that scoundrel, Drake thought. He means to drag me into his filth again.

"Aye, aye, sir. At the service of the King," he replied, then barked at a nearby sailor. "Back to scrubbing, you miserable bilge rat!"

Morgrave clapped Drake's shoulder with the camaraderie of a wolf. "Time to bring justice to this dump, like we did with the Frogs and the Caribs down Tobago way."

Drake raised his hand quickly to silence him before the crew heard more. Morgrave's giddy mood was giving him indigestion.

"Get your dress blues in order. I want the full show today."

"Aye, aye." Drake saluted, suppressing a scowl.

Ten minutes later, the reluctantly uniformed Captain Drake fell in step beside Morgrave. "May I ask the nature of the Crown's business?"

"This is all you need to know." Morgrave pulled a letter from his black patent leather satchel with a freshly pressed royal seal on it. He waved it in the air like a flag for anyone to see and said loudly, "A royal decree from the King himself I am determined to serve."

Before Drake could inspect it, Morgrave tucked it back into his satchel. A team of black horses pulled a dark lacquered carriage that appeared to all like the hearse usually parked under an old sail-cloth behind the graveyard shed. The driver was a man drafted from the Buck and Barrel for a shilling or two.

The sun was high enough to make the cobbles glare when Skip was summoned from the ship to serve as carriage footman. He sulked at the rear step, gripping the rail as if it might gallop away without him. Lord Goodwin Morgrave, of course, had claimed the seat of distinction inside the polished coach, its lacquered panels flashing like dark water in the sun. The door bore no crest, only the smug authority of its occupant. Captain Drake had been ordered to walk ahead, setting the pace like a man leading a parade no one had asked for.

"To the Vincents," Morgrave declared, and climbed into the carriage.

From a distance, the small procession looked like the hearse was bound for a funeral more than a royal visit—two men in solemn stride before a silent coach. Skip, the footman trudging behind like a mournful shadow. Morgrave held his papers in plain view, the false royal seal catching every glint of sunlight as if to blind anyone who dared question him.

Along the way, shopkeepers paused in their

doorways. Mrs. Gunton, the baker's wife, leaned out to watch from her stoop, her flour-dusted arms folded. "Royal business, no doubt," she whispered to Mrs. Pimm beside her.

"Or someone's about to fall from grace," Mrs. Pimm murmured back. Neither named a soul, but their eyes followed Morgrave as though they could divine the culprit by the set of his shoulders.

Drake said nothing, though his jaw was tight. He had been summoned, not invited, and the warm summer air seemed colder for it.

Beth stood in the cottage kitchen, watching Martha pace outside. The girl's steps were tight, deliberate — not the dreamy meandering of a child lost in thought. Something was wrong.

Then Beth saw the damp footprints. They came in from the back door, circled the kitchen, and went back out. Had she been outside all night?

Moments later, Martha reentered, her face pale and her eyes swollen.

Beth had returned to the hearth, working on a torn hem, "Oh my dear!" She froze, the needle suspended mid-stitch, "You've been walking in your sleep again!"

Martha nodded slowly. "But this wasn't just a dream, Auntie. It felt real as you and me." She shuddered, "I saw them—the people, crowds marching to the cliffs. And I saw him, Auntie. I saw Moshup. He looked at me as if he knew who I was."

Beth suppressed her astonishment. "Moshup?"

"He said the island remembers me."

Beth set her work aside, her expression half awe, half fear. "You must tell Pashanok and Wampanuit. Dreams like that are not accidents."

"It was so real, Auntie . . ." Martha watched closely for Beth's reaction, " . . . or should I say, 'Mother'?"

"Martha!" You know you mustn't call me that," Beth cautioned, "I've told you so many times, I knew her—but that person has been dead and long gone now."

Martha wiped the tears away and stared directly into Beth's eyes, then began to describe her dream-vision. She expounded on every detail leading up to Elizabeth's transition from a radiant red-haired beauty into the woman standing before her now, tears streaming down her cheeks.

"I am not some little girl to be soothed with fairy tales, Mother!" Martha felt more empowered every time she spoke the word.

Beth was visibly shaken. How could Martha have known? Did Pashanok betray her trust? No. This was something more—something spiritual. The world tilted, as though she were fleeing aboard that cursed ship once again. She grasped the table behind her as the room began to spin, trying to maintain balance. When she saw Martha's widening eyes it tripped the balance and with a heavy gasp her knees buckled as she collapsed against the table, fainting into the chair.

When she finally recovered, she was on her bed with Martha leaning over her, weeping and kissing her face again and again.. "Mother! Mother! I'm so sorry! Please! Please wake up! Please!"

The emotion was so unabashedly deep and honest,

the love so pure and kind, she raised her hands and cupped Martha's face and replied, "You are right, Martha. I am Elizabeth—your mother. You must know why I said those things—I love you more than life itself. I am the one who should be sorry—not you my sweet child."

Martha smiled so broadly it hurt. Her heart leapt with joy like a spring lamb. They clung to one another, as if meeting for the first time.

The moment ebbed and each retreated to their own thoughts, wondering where their lives might lead. Beth hoped Martha would understand without a long explanation, but that wasn't to be. The girl was overflowing with questions, and smart ones at that, but she held back.

Martha's joy gave way to confusion. "Why have you lied to me for all these years? You said my mother died! What's so horrible about the truth? What's wrong with me, that you would rather be my aunt than my mother? You're ashamed of me, aren't you!"

Beth tried to speak, but Martha surged forward, hurt rising like a tide. "It wasn't just a lie. It feels like—*like I embarrass you!*"

Martha's emotions were gathering steam, the pressure of years of memories building up within her; moments when Beth kept her emotional distance for fear of getting too close as 'Auntie'.

"No, No, No! Martha! . . . I . . ." Beth begged.

But Martha wouldn't listen, couldn't listen.

"Please!" She shouted. "You lied! You—you've been using me!"

She couldn't hear any explanation now for fear it

would be another lie. She had to find someone who could help her sort this out, someone who would know and be bold with the truth. Some voice in the back of her mind said, "You will know the truth and it will set you free." and freedom was the only thing she needed just then—even if it meant breaking her mother's heart. She ran out the door and up the path to the lane with her mother chasing after her, crying out—

"MARTHA! PLEASE COME BACK! PLEASE DON'T GO! . . . you're . . . all . . . I . . . have left . . . "

Martha was determined now. She ran barefoot, just as she'd been in the dream, to her vineyard where she could breathe, where truth lived. She longed for it's soft grasses and sweet fragrances; the embrace of the vines. *Her mother was not dead after all!*

Lord Goodwin Morgrave and Captain Drake stood before the Vincent estate. A maid answered and summoned her mistress.

"I am here on royal business," Lord Morgrave declared, waving his falsified decree like a banner. "Under the King's authority."

Mrs. Vincent, pale and trembling, led them to the parlor dabbing a kerchief to her brow. Drake sat, trying not to wince at her distress. Morgrave remained standing, smug.

"I am tasked with pursuing traitors to the Crown—and those who harbor them. The penalty for aiding such criminals is severe. The King gives quarter to no one, no matter their station in life." He folded his arms, glaring.

Mrs. Vincent gasped, clutching the cross at her neck.

Captain Drake shifted in his seat, wishing he was back aboard his ship.

Morgrave turned to the window, savoring her fear.

"I seek a woman by the name of Elizabeth Vincent." The surname "Vincent" on the decree was a major strategic invention Morgrave was quite proud of. Even the Captain was shocked by the audacity of his direct accusation.

Mrs. Vincent began to cry.

Mr. Vincent entered, alerted from his office by her distress. "What is the meaning of this? Who are you to make my wife weep in her own parlor?" He turned to her, "You may go dear, I will handle these rude, uncouth men!"

"You are facing a charge of treason by collaboration, Richard Abraham Vincent!" Morgrave roared, slamming the fake decree onto the table. "Behave as if the King himself were here or I will have you in irons!"

Captain Drake, caught in the charade, gave a stiff nod.

Mrs. Vincent fled crying down the hallway past Edgar who was listening intently just outside the door.

Gaining momentum, Morgrave waved the fake decree once again, now more confident in his scheme. "Elizabeth Vincent is wanted by the King and his court for theft of royal items totaling over ten thousand pounds, to include but not limited to a gold locket, a royal signet ring, estate deeds and documents of laden for a ship of the line. Captain Drake here, of the Royal Navy will verify and attest to the fidelity of these documents.

Richard Vincent bristled. "This is nonsense."

"Your wife knew her. She's kept it from you, I can see it in her eyes. Shall I drag her to court for lying to the King?"

But before he could continue, the older head housekeeper—Mildred—cleared her throat. All eyes went to her.

"If it please your Lordship," she said nervously, "I think I can explain."

"Speak now woman!" He ordered.

"It twas nigh-on ten years past, m'Lord, maybe more. I remember because we had a horrible bout of the pox here on the island. It was before the honorable Mr. Vincent and his family arrived, I swear on the Holy Bible, I do." She nodded to her employer and master. "She was a most brilliant young woman with blazing curly red hair and sparkling blue eyes. Somehow she was befriended by the late Caroline Mayhew and . . ." Her voice cracked and she began to sniffle.

"Get on with it! I have no time for blubbering!" Morgrave insisted.

"It's okay Mildred, please continue." Mr. Vincent patted her back gently.

"Well, the pox was delivered by some ship up from New Amsterdam, quarantined in the harbor by Reverend Mayhew. But didn't some poor souls escape who thought they were healthy and poor Mrs. Mayhew took them and their children in at the orphanage. And didn't Satan give her the plague as a result, and poor Reverend Mayhew! His own wife lost for the crime of compassion . . . poor thing! That Elizabeth stuck by her side until the bitter end . . .

caught the pox herself and the day after Caroline died, God rest her soul, she flat out disappeared. Gone to the wind."

Morgrave seized on the name and snapped his fingers, "Mayhew".

"She was here, m'Lord. But she caught the pox. Disappeared the day after poor Caroline died."

Morgrave retrieved a gold locket from his vest pocket and flipped it open, "Is this the young woman you speak of? Is this her?"

She looked over at Mr. Vincent who nodded, "Yes M'Lord, that is she . . . or was . . ."

Morgrave turned to Drake. "To the church," he barked.

As they left, Drake offered the Vincents a small, apologetic bow.

Edgar ran down the hallway and slipped out the back door, running to warn Martha and Beth about Morgrave's mission. Skip, grinning in the shadows, followed him like a hunter tracks his prey . . . back to that cottage no doubt.

— *Chapter 12* —

Martha's vineyard lay hushed beneath the late-morning sun, the rows of vines heavy with purple-green clusters. Here, among the whisper of leaves and the low hum of bees, she felt the world's noise fall away. The faint scent of sun-warmed wool from the dyed skeins hung on the fence drifted in the air, mingling with the earthy sweetness of ripening grapes. She traced her fingers along a curling tendril, watching how it clung without hesitation, certain of its place.

She rose and crossed to her special box of collections, prizing open the lid as though it held the island's secrets. From the wampum shell, the feather, and the pebble smoothed by tide, she made space near the coin and laid Edgar's rose blossom gently within. Its pink was already fading, and with it the hope of his eyes at the harbor, yet Beth's stern warning against him returned sharper than ever. The thought stung—why should something so small and kind be forbidden?

Her mind, restless, reached for another memory. She saw Auntie Beth in the garden one twilight, hands folded in her lap, shoulders trembling as though the earth itself had let her down. Martha had crept near and asked why she wept, and Beth whispered of her mother far away in England. Without hesitation, Martha pressed against her and said, "Auntie Beth, you can be my mother." Beth had drawn a sharp breath, eyes shining, and whispered back with a tremor she quickly tried to hide, "I just might be after all."

Her attention turned to Pashanok and the **wuttawâm** he would surely know. There were so many things she needed to ask—things she had a right to know now. Had he known her mother before the sickness? What had she been like as a girl in England? Why had she left— and why had she stayed? Had Pashanok seen her the day she first came ashore? Did he know what she carried with her, and what she'd left behind?

Each question made her step quicker in her imagination, pushing her toward the man who had been both guardian and gatekeeper. She wanted the truth of her mother's name, the truth of her own, and the story of how the woman called Beth had become who she was now.

Her chest felt light and tight at once. She gathered her resolve, drawing one last breath of the vineyard's stillness before stepping onto the lane.

Martha pushed herself harder along the winding lane, feet pounding the dusty earth. The shock of the morning still clung to her—the dream, the truth, her mother's collapse. Finally, after years of mystery, years of questions: *The Truth*. Why was that so hard? She felt free, emboldened. It was time to confront Pashanok now, to learn what he knew about Elizabeth . . . things she still may hold in secret.

As she continued, musing to herself, she heard a faint

moan. There, just off the road in a tangled patch of brambles, lay a little African girl. Daisy!

Her dress was torn, and her lip was split. Bruises darkened her arms and face. She stirred slightly at Martha's voice, lifted her head just slightly and gave way to exhaustion.

"Oh no—NO! Daisy! Daisy, it's me—Martha. I've got you."

She knelt, lifting the girl's head, brushing dirt and leaves away with trembling fingers.

"Who did this to you? Why? Oh my God, Why!"

Daisy's voice was barely a whisper. "Daisies . . . in your hair . . . I liked . . ." A tiny smile flickered over her lips, replaced by low voice of terror. "Run! Now! . . . GO! . . . selling . . . the . . . selling!" She drifted off and lost consciousness in fearful spasms.

Tears stung Martha's eyes. She saw fragments of daisy petals in her hair and a fury rose in her heart like a burning fire. She grit her teeth and shook her fist in the air., "They will pay for this. Mark my words!".

She hoisted Daisy as best she could and began the long, slow walk toward the Wampanoag camp. Every step dug into her feet, her arms burning from Daisy's weight, but she pressed on.

Martha crossed into the camp, and to them, she was Môsi—warmly spoken with familial welcome. Children stopped playing. A mother dropped her bundle of herbs.

"Help! Please! She's hurt!"

Two women rushed to take Daisy. Pashanok emerged from the gathering circle and hurried to Môsi's side.

"She needs—healing," Môsi gasped. "They left her for dead. Because she dared to be human. Dared to be a sweet little girl."

Pashanok placed a steadying hand on Môsi's shoulder, but his gaze swept the camp. The arrival of a stranger had already drawn a small crowd—women with baskets of shellfish on their hips, children darting in to stare before being shooed back. Argon padded close at Martha's side, head low, his hackles just enough to warn anyone from pressing too near.

Tobiasquash stood at the edge of the circle, a spear in hand from the morning's fishing, watching with a mix of curiosity and quiet pride.

One of the older women clicked her tongue. "She is not of our blood," she muttered in Wôpanâak. "Better to take her back to her own people."

Another voice, sharper: "Why bring trouble into the camp? Her sickness may follow her."

Môsi stiffened, heat rising in her chest. Argon pressed against her leg, as if lending his weight to hers. "We are all her people," she said, her voice carrying more authority than she meant it to. "She has no one but us."

The murmurs quieted. Some turned away, unwilling to meet her eyes. Others lingered, studying her as if weighing the truth of her words.

Pashanok's expression didn't change, but the faintest glint warmed his eyes. He inclined his head toward the medicine shelter, speaking low so only she could hear. "You speak as one who belongs everywhere," he said.

"Now, let us see what can be done."

With that, he guided her toward Wampanuit's wetu, Argon padded along beside them. Tobiasquash fell into step a few paces back, the crowd parting just enough to let them pass.

The **powwaw** , Wampanuit, appeared moments later. He knelt beside Daisy, examined her wounds, then gave a sharp command in Wôpanâak. Women disappeared into separate clan wetus. Smoke rose as salves and poultices were prepared.

Inside, the warm dense air smelled of cedar and crushed herbs. Wampanuit glanced up from his work, his dark eyes narrowing in quick assessment of the child. He motioned for Môsi to set Daisy on a mat near the hearth.

Argon circled once, lying down just far enough to watch without getting in the way.

Pashanok spoke briefly to Wampanuit in low Wôpanâak, then stepped outside with Tobiasquash. The younger man waited until the flap had closed before speaking.

"You see her full spirit now," Tobiasquash murmured, nodding toward the wetu. "She's not only Auntie Beth's girl. She speaks as one of us."

Pashanok's mouth twitched, not quite a smile. "She has always been one of us, Tobiasquash. The others will learn."

"And if they do not?"

Pashanok looked toward the path leading to the village, his jaw set. "Then she will stand between them, as she did today. And we will stand beside her."

Tobiasquash shifted his spear, glancing back at the shelter. "I would follow her into any fight. Even without my weapons."

"That," Pashanok said, resting a hand on his nephew's shoulder, "is the only weapon she truly needs."

The small crowd hushed as they gathered outside the weti, listening to the murmur of Wampanuit's supplicant chants to Keesoq and the healing spirits. All eyes were on Môsi as she came from the confined atmosphere of the healing ceremony. Pashanok gently assisted her to an opening where she could rest. She nodded to those who understood her deep concern for Daisy. The dam of her emotions finally gave way to a flood of tears. She collapsed into Pashanok's arms, the weight of the day finally too great to carry alone. A girl brought her water. She took long deep gulps as she watched for someone to announce Daisy's condition.

Pashanok ducked inside for a moment and returned. "She is frightened and very weak, but she will live."

"She's brave," Môsi said. "She had nowhere to run. But she came to find me."

There was a long silence.

"Why would someone do this!" she stated more than asked.

Pashanok's voice was low. "Fear. Power. Some men become more like beasts, worse than animals, when they believe no one will stop them."

Môsi took Pashanok by the elbow and turned him to face her. She looked him directly in the eye. "We need to talk."

She gathered her strength, brushed the grass and dirt from her dress and led him to a private spot on the cliffs overlooking the harbor. A long silence followed as she measured her thoughts, and he observed her spirit.

This wasn't the Môsi he was used to. She had the determination of an adult—now a woman who knew her own worth, understood her own power. She had a clarity of spirit that carried the drive for truth.

Môsi began solemnly, describing a sacred moment in her life.

"Last night a beautiful red-haired woman came to me in a dream. She transformed into Auntie Beth before my eyes. I confronted her this morning, and she finally told me the truth. She is my mother. She was that beautiful woman—Elizabeth, years ago—before I was born. But I need to know more! Why has she lied to me all these years? Why have you lied to me about her?"

Pashanok answered calmly. "We haven't lied to you, Martha. We were waiting for the right time to tell you. Keesoq lights the path of truth when the season is right. That season is now."

He paused, choosing each word with care.

"Elizabeth came sick and starving from the sea. I found her on the beach, tangled in seaweed, her skin burned, her breath a thread. I carried her to Wampanuit, who drew her back from the edge of death. During that time, I fell in love with her—as she did with me. We shared everything from our hearts until nothing was left hidden."

"Then I pleaded with Reverend Mayhew and Caroline to take her in. As a nanapashômut, she belonged in the village with people of her own language. I kept checking back on her as she built her new life. I visited her quietly, when no one was looking. I did not ask where she came from. I was thankful she had survived."

His eyes softened. "She was like fire. Bold, bright, impossible to hold. She fought with me, laughed with me, loved from the depths of her soul. I thought no one could stop us. And even now… just look how powerful she is. Everything she touches."

Martha listened, her throat tight, her eyes wet. "That was the woman—my mother—in the dream."

Pashanok nodded, voice low but firm. "Yes. And there is more, Martha. She is not the only one bound to you. My blood runs in you as well. I am your father. I have walked in silence with my clan because among our people, bloodline belongs to the mother."

He paused, choosing his words with care.

"When we learned of her pregnancy and it could no longer be hidden, it was Caroline who sheltered her— heavy with child, frightened, and in need of care that could not be given openly. She asked no questions and offered no judgment. She kept watch with deep devotion, as she had from the beginning."

Her father knelt on one knee and took her hands in his. His eyes bore into hers.

"You must know this now: You are my daughter too, Môsi. You are of me, as surely as you are of her."

For a moment Martha simply stared, unable to breathe. She wanted so desperately to hug him as she always had. But anger surged up in her, breaking loose at last.

"All this time! All these years you stood before me,

teaching me, guiding me, and I never knew! You let me believe I was fatherless! That I was—nothing but a burden to you!" Her voice cracked as she turned away..

"You were both right there—right there!—*and I was alone.*"

Her chest heaved as her eyes darted between past and present, memory and revelation. "Every time you looked at me, you knew. Every time she brushed my hair, she knew. And you said nothing! Not to me. Not once!"

Pashanok's jaw clenched, his eyes wet with restrained grief.

Martha turned back to him, trembling, the words tumbled out of her. "We live such separate lives. We live without you, Pashanok. Father! Do you hear me? *Father!* You belong to your clan, your family. She aches for you every day, and I ache for what I never had! And we—she and I—we have no one but each other. No one but shadows."

Her voice fell to a whisper. "You do not know what it feels like to have both your parents, and yet be— orphaned in your own home!"

Pashanok let her words crash over him like storm surf against the cliffs. He did not flinch. He let her see his eyes, steady and unguarded, so she would know the weight of his truth.

"My daughter," he said slowly, "you are right to be angry. You are right to feel the ache of what was withheld. I have felt it too—every day I walked past you and did not claim you, every time I saw her hands tremble when she longed to call you daughter instead of child. That wound is real. I will not pretend it is not."

He stepped closer, lowering his voice until it felt like the two of them were sealed in a circle apart from the world.

"But hear me: we did not hide you because we were ashamed. We hid you because the world is cruel. A girl of two peoples, too strong for one side and too proud for the other—they would have torn you apart. They would have made you a pawn of their quarrels, or worse, taken you far away. To keep you safe, we bore the lie ourselves. We carried its weight, so you could grow without it crushing you."

Martha's lips parted, ready to rail again—but no words came. His steadiness pulled the wind from her sails. For the first time, she felt the enormity of their sacrifice, and it pressed against her anger like a hand cooling a fever. She turned away, blinking fast, her chest still heaving but no longer with fury alone. His hand hovered, then rested lightly over her heart.

"You are not less for it. You are more. In you flows the strength of both worlds, the sea and the shore, the English tongue and the Wampanoag tongue, the fire of Elizabeth and the patience of Pashanok. One day, when truth cannot be hidden, this will not be a burden. It will be your weapon. Your gift."

He lifted his gaze toward the sky, "Keesoq—the Great Spirit—shows itself only when the world is ready to receive it. So too has your truth been kept until now. And now you see it. Now you carry it. Not as shame, Martha, but as power."

He rubbed her shoulder softly. "Think of that dream you had again. How did your mother look at the end?"

"She shed the diseased skin on her face so that her inner brightness shone like the sun. So bright that I could still see her with my eyes closed!" Môsi said, amazement in her voice. "What does that mean?"

"Listen to your heart. You know what it means. It is the truth about her spirit—and her love for you."

Môsi whispered, "But I want to be angry. Yet all I feel is—sorrow. For her. For what she lost."

"You're right, Môsi. Truth is woven through our lives and everything around us. Keesoq gives us all we need, but not always what we want. To know and understand the truth? We need to be listening constantly—to hear and observe where and how we fit into this vine-complicated world."

He tried to explain. "All of us are constantly learning, no matter our age. I know that's hard to hear when older ones seem to know it all. The fact is, we don't always seek what will be best for us in the long time."

"I understand that. I do." Môsi nodded, then her brow furrowed. "But there were other things in my dream—people marching off the Aquinnah cliffs to the sound of a war drum, and they wouldn't stop. And then—" She hesitated. "Then he appeared in the air. He said *Noepe remembers me.*"

Pashanok placed a hand on her head gently, knowing whom she spoke of. "When Moshup shows himself, it is not to frighten, and not to command. It is because Noepe is speaking through someone who can hear it. There is something ancient moving in you, my little one— something with a destiny only time will tell. We will walk together every step of the way—as a family."

Pashanok looked to the ocean. He rested his hand at her back, and for the first time as her father, did not feel the need to stand apart.

"This is where you are meant to be," he said quietly. "Noepe knows you."

"Forever," she said.

Later, as shadows lengthened, Martha left the camp alone. Her footsteps were slower now, heavy with thought. She let the silence of the forest guide her. Sunlight slipped through the canopy in golden threads.

Every step felt heavier than the last. She had wanted the truth all her life, and now that it was hers, it pressed on her chest like a stone. Her mother was not lost. Her father was not absent. They had been with her all along, guarding her in shadows, shaping every part of who she was. Yet somehow, that knowledge did not lift her; it bound her tighter.

The lie had not been told to her, she realized. It had been told for her. And now she carried it, too. The secret was no longer theirs alone but hers to protect, a fire she must keep hidden under her own cloak. She felt both older and younger in the same breath—a child aching for the years of closeness denied, and a young woman suddenly conscripted into the burdens of her parents.

The forest whispered no answers, only the rustle of leaves and the distant call of crows returning to their roosts. She folded her arms across her chest as if to hold the secret inside her, as if to remind herself that it was not weakness, but power—just as Pashanok had said.

— *Chapter 13* —

Martha saw Edgar's horse at the edge of the clearing, its reins trailing as it grazed among the weeds. Beth sat on the cottage step, her shoulders bowed, her clasped hands twisting the washcloth in her lap. Edgar paced in front of her, his brow furrowed, worry written across his young face.

When he spotted Martha, he rushed forward, words tumbling out. "I—I came to warn you. About that Lord Morgrave. He was at my house today. He knows about Auntie Beth—her past in England. He called her a traitor to the Crown. And he has—he showed us—a decree from the King himself!"

Martha froze, her breath catching. Out of the corner of her eye she saw Beth look away, pale and trembling, though she held her chin high.

"Don't worry Auntie Beth." Martha forced the words past the knot in her throat. She stumbled slightly over Auntie, wishing she could say Mother, but Edgar's presence made her bite it back.

"It must be some trick." She folded her arms tight across her chest, her voice firmer than she felt. "It must be a scheme to frighten us. We'll go to Reverend Mayhew. He'll know what to do."

Beth's eyes flickered toward her, just for an instant —

a silent recognition of the word unsaid. Her fingers stilled on her skirt, smoothing it as she rose, shoulders squared against the weight of the moment. She gave the slightest shake of her head, a plea only Martha would notice. Then she steadied her voice.

"That's not a bad idea. The church is sanctuary. And the Reverend—he is Constable too. We'll reason this out, put it to rest once and for all."

At that they heard the sharp snap of a twig that came from the path to town, followed by the sound of someone running away.

Beth already had Edgar's horse by the reins, "You don't mind if I ride him back into the village, do you Edgar!"

It wasn't a request.

"Of course you can!" Edgar was eager to help as he offered his hand up for her.

Before anything more could be said, Beth was gone—riding bareback like a born equestrian.

"I just hope she beats that turncoat Skip to the church!" Edgar deeply regretted ever meeting his new 'friend'.

Beth slowed the horse at the edge of town and dismounted. She couldn't afford to draw attention at this crucial moment. As she rounded the corner to approach the church she saw Skip banging on the church door, breathless with excitement. She saw Captain Drake open it and heard a commotion inside, wishing she knew what was said.

He had caught Skip by the shirt as he rushed by. "She's there at that cottage I told you about! The white-haired woman! That's her! And she's—"

Captain Drake had enough with this Morgrave scheme and his little whelp, Skip. "Go back to the ship, boy, before I have you whipped for insolence. You won't have me chasing pell-mell around this God forsaken island after ghosts and white-haired witches!"

"But—I'm telling you! She's—"

Drake twisted him out the door. "NOW!"

Skip slunk away, grumbling. "They'll regret it, not listening to me!"

Beth watched Skip kicking stones as he headed for the ship. She sneaked through the bushes past the rectory to the back of the church, hoping to find a quiet place to wait for Reverend Mayhew. She opened the door stealthily and slipped inside.

Morgrave confronted the Reverend. "Then where is she? Where is Elizabeth Vincent?"

Mayhew folded his hands calmly. "She was not of the Vincent family, and she died of the pox, Lord Morgrave. The woman you think you're looking for is long gone."

Morgrave reached into his coat and pulled out the locket. "And this? Explain this!"

Mayhew leaned forward, eyes narrowing. "That belonged to Elizabeth, yes. Where did you get it?"

Morgrave snapped the locket shut. "It was claimed by some savage. Likely stolen. Like everything else on this cursed island."

With a sweeping gesture Mayhew said, "There's no fugitive Elizabeth here, Lord Morgrave.   Look for yourself." Confident that Beth wasn't in the church, Mayhew invited Morgrave to search the entire property as proof.

And as fate would have it, the first door he opened found a frightened Beth with her white hair unbound, veil forgotten, eyes wide in panic. She nearly collided with him trying to flee.

"YOU!" Morgrave snarled.

Beth screamed, "NO!" twisted away and ran for the front door.

Drake, still at the door, grabbed her arm, his expression pained. "Forgive me," he said calmly. "I must— follow orders."

The midday sun glared off the cobbles as the black lacquered hearse creaked along Dock Street, its polished panels swallowing the light like deep water. Captain Drake walked at the head of the procession, his face set in a grim, unreadable mask. Inside, Lord Goodwin Morgrave lounged in the seat of honor, gloved hands resting on his knees as if he were presiding over a private court.

Chained to the rear axle, Beth stumbled to keep pace, the iron biting her wrists and sending dull shocks of pain up her arms. Her white hair streamed behind her, catching in the breeze like a tattered flag, a pale ghost trailing the hearse-like coach. Skip rode the foot-board at the back, grinning back down at her with all the malice he could muster. Every few paces, he spat carelessly, the drops darkening the dust near her feet.

From shop doorways and stoops, faces turned to watch. The two graveyard gossips stood front and center by the apothecary, their eyes bright with the thrill of scandal. "A thief, no doubt," one said. "And worse," the other replied. "I've heard she calls the wind to do her bidding." A knot of fishermen leaned on a barrel, muttering their superstitions, while a boy pointed and laughed until his mother pulled him inside. Beth kept her gaze forward, her jaw tight, her dignity clinging to her like the last threadbare scrap of a once-fine gown. With each grueling step toward the wharf, the chains rattled like a tolling bell.

The merchants watched as she was led down Dock Street, wrists shackled, white hair flowing.

"Witch!" A cruel girl sneered. "Mark my words! She will burn!"

Beth's eyes brimmed with tears, but she did not lower her head. Morgrave stepped down from the carriage and made a show of strutting back to his captive. Her outward display of defiance felt to him like a deep stab to his pride. He struck the back of her legs with his riding crop and she fell to her knees. Lord Goodwin Morgrave took her by the chains and dragged her across the gravel of the half-built wharf.

Martha and Edgar stopped short outside the church. The spectacle of Morgrave marching Beth down Dock Street in chains behind the black carriage struck them with dread. Edgar had to hold Martha back with all his strength as she lunged, twisted and fought to pursue the tyrant Morgrave and gouge his eyes out.

"M—" The word caught in her throat before it fully

left her lips. Not Auntie, not Beth—the word she wanted most was the one she couldn't speak here. Beth's eyes found Martha's in the chaos, a single sharp shake of her head: not here, not now. It cut through Martha's fury like a lash, the silent command of a mother who had always known when words would be too dangerous.

Martha twisted in Edgar's grip, fighting like a trapped animal. Edgar strained to hold her, but Martha's strength shocked even herself. For the first time, she felt taller than she was, stronger than she should be, as though the truth of who she was lent fire to her limbs.

The commanding voice of Reverend Mayhew standing on the church steps jolted them to attention, "Get over here you two, RIGHT NOW!" They ran to him and were quickly ushered into the church.

"We don't have much time, so we'll have to work quickly, the ship is scheduled to sail on the next tide, tonight." Reverend Mayhew said in the gravest of tones. "There's no telling what Morgrave has in mind, but whatever it is, he's determined to get his reward."

"But Reverend Mayhew! You're the Constable here, You can demand sanctuary for her and take her back, can't you!" Martha pleaded.

"I'm afraid the time for that is over." He lamented. "Now that she's aboard The Deliverance she's in their custody and I'm powerless to set her free."

Martha and Edgar looked at each other in disbelief. How could this happen, and right before their eyes? Their attitude began to shift from fear to determination.

The Reverend saw this and warned, "I see what you're thinking. You two better leave this to me. I mean it.

Now go home and get your things in order. Beth will need you to be strong for her."

"Okay Reverend Mayhew. That's what we'll do." Martha said in all seriousness as they slowly backed down the church steps.

Just down the street, Martha turned to Edgar with a smile and winked.

She had a plan.

— Chapter 14 —

Martha and Edgar trudged their way back to the Vincent estate in deep thought, Martha conjuring the details of her plan while Edgar recalled the days events. They had retrieved his horse and were sitting on a bale of hay outside the barn while a heath hen pecked at insects in the straw.

Edgar kept his eyes on the ground, turning a pebble with his boot, pondering his fate. He couldn't shake the thought of his father's stern face, or what would happen if word spread that he was mixed up in this. Harboring fugitives? Defying the Crown? Defying his own family?—it could ruin the Vincents, and land Martha under the cruel hand of Ms. Hawkins at the orphanage. The thought twisted his stomach.

Beside him, Martha sat rigid, staring past the fence line toward the distant lane. Her guilt pressed harder than her fear. She had lashed out at Beth, called her words hateful, and fled like a child. And now Beth was gone—dragged away in chains—without a chance to mend what she'd broken. Love and regret knotted together in her chest until she could hardly breathe. All she knew was that she couldn't let their life end like that. What would happen to the cottage and the animals? To Moses? To Argon? She set her mind on one purpose and steeled her resolve.

"We have to get on board that ship!" Martha burst out.

"Yes. But we can't go up the dock." Edgar shook his head, "There will be guards."

"So we have to climb up the side somewhere—and soon!" She groaned. "Reverend Mayhew said they're leaving tonight on the next tide!"

"We don't even know where they're holding her." Edgar sulked. "This is impossible, Martha."

A new thought sparked in her like a lightning bolt, and she could barely contain her excitement. "I know exactly what we'll do!"

"Whatever you need, Martha. Auntie Beth is like family to me too!"

She smiled and patted his shoulder, "We have work to do!"

That night, the gibbous moon lifted over the horizon like a pale, watchful eye. On the wharf below, sailors moved in the half-light, their voices low as they hauled lines and trimmed sails in preparation for departure. The scent of tar and brine drifted through the still air, mingling with the faint creak of timbers. Somewhere out in the darkness, a gull cried, its voice sharp and lonely. Shadows swayed across the deck as lanterns were hung, each glow a small reminder that the ship would not sleep before dawn.

Lord Morgrave took childish delight in his wicked teasing once he had Beth shackled to a ship's beam in his state-room closet. He now wore her locket around his neck and dangled it in her face.

"Look at the beauty now! People calling her 'Witch'! HO! HO! HO! How fitting!" He pointed through the porthole at the colorful sunset and laughed diabolically, "Your life sets with the sun."

He waved his forged royal decree, looping it in the air, "And this isn't even real!" He roared with laughter again.

She spat at him but missed.

Lord Morgrave paused before leaving and trilled in a creepy soft voice, "Goodwin shall return, my dear."

She heard him chuckling to himself on the way out the door.

The warm glow of the sunset, yellow, peach and orange gave way to red, purple and blue until dusk became twilight. Beth sat uncomfortably in the storage closet against the beam she was chained to, her arms above her head chafing sorely at the irons around her wrists. She had worn through the skin trying to pull free and now she felt drops of blood dampening the sleeves of her dress.

Memories of her only other ship passage came flooding back, with that same demonic Morgrave voice only much younger, ringing in her ears. "We will get this Elizabeth Montgomery!" He used to storm back and forth cursing on deck while she hid below. This time she was captured for a certainty.

She couldn't allow the fear to overcome hope. She believed this was not her fate as she had before, but sadly, she was humbled once again.

From the shadow of the pier, Martha crouched low, her eyes fixed on a thick drift log resting half in the water. She pushed it silently into the harbor, wading knee-deep until the tide caught it. The salt stung her eyes, but she kept her grip, kicking gently to guide it between the bobbing hulls. Lantern light spilled from a dozen decks above, casting wavering gold across the dark water. She slipped into the cool silence between two anchored schooners, letting the swell carry her closer to the looming shape of the *Deliverance*.

Martha swam hidden alongside the giant log until she reached the ship's shadowed flank. She cupped a hand to her mouth and gave a low, lilting call—the whistle of the **pâwâhsuw**—whippoorwill.

On the other side of the ship, Edgar heard her signal and pulled a cart loaded with his father's wine and rum up to the end of the dock.

Skip dropped the line he was coiling and waved, then turned to a few sailors nearby, "Ahoy Mates! It's Edgar Vincent! My friend comes bearing gifts for the voyage!"

One sailor came forward and spoke in a low tone, "Aye Skipper my boy. Hush now 'fore the Cap'n catches wind and takes all that grog!"

Another leaned on the rail. "First mate will tattle for sure. Let's make quick work of it then!"

Edgar had no idea what they would do, so long as he could keep their attention away from Martha. He heard the whippoorwill call again. He clapped his hands loudly so she could hear.

The few sailors carrying bottles jumped in surprise, "Hey now laddie!" One said in a hoarse whisper, "Don't ye be giving us away now! Hush up with yer clappin'."

Edgar nodded, "Sorry sir. I'll not do it again."

"There's a good boy." Another said, an open bottle in one hand, the cork in his teeth.

Beth felt sick to her stomach, her nerves at the very end. For all she had endured, all that she built, all that she sacrificed, now this? She fought back her fear with one solid truth: Martha was safe with Pashanok now. Her own foolish, impetuous past wouldn't handicap her daughter ever again. However she might pay in this life and the next, at least she could rest knowing Martha would fulfill her destiny as a powerful intelligent woman.

She closed her eyes and rested her head against the beam that held her. Then a faint whistle broke the silence. Beth couldn't believe it. Was that the . . . pâwâhsuw?

Martha had an idea that Beth was being kept somewhere deep below-decks near the dank rat infested bilge. She thumped her log against the hull and ducked below the water when a sailor looked over the rail. She rose finally when he lost interest and listened for some kind of response. Nothing.

She gave the pâwâhsuw call again.

Edgar was quickly losing control as the sailors began to fight over who would carry the liquor and where they might hide it on board. One popped a cork, another heard and did the same. Soon a dozen men on the dock and aboard the ship were chugging rum and wine like there was no tomorrow.

"Set sail be damned." Skip shouted and they all laughed, until a musket shot boomed, echoing across the harbor.

First Mate Trumbull lowered his gun. He brought a whistle to his lips, gave a few short blasts and shouted the order: "All hands on deck! Muster for inspection by order of Captain Drake!"

A great rumble of men ensued from all over the ship. Those down below were rousted from their hammocks and those in the rigging above came down like hail stones, landing on the deck. Bottles broke on the wharf and splashed overboard as the crew ditched contraband as fast as they could.

Skip tucked as many bottles as he could under his tunic and fled to Morgrave's quarters. He knew his master would be pleased, but he wasn't there.

Beth's heart raced. The pâwâhsuw! It had to be Pashanok!

That was his private signal to her, always had been since they first began secretly courting. She remembered hearing it outside her window at the Mayhew's house. She immediately called back, hoping he'd hear her through the porthole.

But the next moment, terror followed. If it was Pashanok… they would surely kill him.

Morgrave heard the gunshot and immediately headed for the Captain's stateroom to reprimand him for disturbing the peace. Once on deck he witnessed the First Mate stomping his foot while screaming at the crew.

Captain Drake made his appearance and the ship fell silent.

Martha pushed the log ahead of her, scraping along the hull towards the stern where she heard the faint bird-call response. She wanted to whoop in joy, but now came the hard part, climbing up the rudder chains into the hull and then pull off her rescue without being seen. It was madness, but what choice did she have?

In the silence, the entire crew heard what seemed to be the third or fourth trill of a whippoorwill. The Captain, muttered loud enough for half the assembled sailors to hear, "What the blazes is with this flock of songbirds tonight!"

"Must be the moon, Captain." said the First Mate.

"Or it's the savages." The cook casually mumbled to himself.

"The WHAT?" Captain Drake growled. "Explain yourself Cookie!"

"Or the savages, sir." The cook gestured bird wings with his hands, "You know, when they're on the . . . "

"HUNT." Morgrave's voice boomed from the starboard rail. "Be on the lookout for savages! They may be on board now!"

This sent the crew scrambling to general quarters. Each had their own specific wartime role. Some went for swords while others to the muskets. Those with neither grabbed a belaying pin in each hand, ready to fight.

Beth heard the First Mate's whistle, the silence, the Captain's voice and the last pâwâhsuw call. Then Morgrave's voice yell "Hunt!" followed by another whistle and then pandemonium topside.

She dreaded the implications of what might be happening outside. All her hopes for rescue were slowly drowning in a sea of despair. What would Martha do if Pashanok were captured? What would they do to him? Shoot him on sight of course. She shut that thought out of her mind. He was too smart to continue. He would find another way.

"Over here!" A sailor at the stern called. He pointed to a log moving like a shark alongside the hull. Without a thought, another sailor fired his musket into it followed by two or three others.

Down below, Beth cried out, "NOOO! Stop! Please, please STOP!" Her tears flowed down her cheeks as she renewed her struggle against the chains.

Morgrave and the Captain parted those at the stern rail and leaned over to investigate.

A small arm shot up from below the log and a sputtering girl came after it, gasping for air. She immediately dove back under and began swimming away as fast as she could.

The First Mate shouted, "Man overboard!" and four sailors leapt in after her while another cast a line after them.

Despite Martha's speed, she was no match for seasoned sailors who chased her down and caught hold of her.

The first howled in pain, "THE DEVIL! SHE BIT ME!"

The next was beat in the head by a rock she must've taken from the bottom. Both men cursed in panic as though she were some sea-witch clawing from the deep, fighting harder than a girl her size should.

The third held her firm while the fourth wrapped the line around her and cinched it tight, making the signal to haul her aboard.

Beth's tears stopped and her emotions were held in suspense after the gunfire ceased. Then she heard the call "Man overboard!" and wondered what that could mean. A few moments later another commotion began on deck and for the first time in her life the sound of Martha's defiant voice made her sick. The girl began trilling the whippoorwill signal over and over again perhaps as a diversion. Beth gasped in sympathetic pain as a loud 'crack' silenced the girl in an instant.

The door to her prison chamber flung open. Morgrave stood there with the Captain and First Mate behind him, Skip skulking just behind their shadows, eyes darting for scraps of drama. Morgrave dragged Martha's limp body to the threshold and let her slump on the deck, her head lolling to one side.

"Mother—I'm so—sorry," she sighed, the word barely audible before surrendering to unconsciousness.

Beth's heart wrenched. She staggered forward as far as her chains would allow, straining against the iron. For the briefest instant, the mask she had worn for twelve years shattered.

Morgrave's grin spread like a knife wound. He crouched low, and whispered loud enough for all present to hear, "Mother. Did you hear that, Elizabeth? At last the little bird sings the truth. What a lovely family reunion this is."

Beth froze, her silence the only defense left to her.

Morgrave straightened and addressed the others with mocking ceremony. "Gentlemen, behold—the witch and her spawn. Mother and daughter, hiding all these years on this pathetic little island." He let the words linger, savoring the ruin they promised.

Skip's eyes widened at the revelation. He observed Beth with a strange new calculation, as though he'd been handed a coin too valuable to spend. "So the kid is her daughter", he repeated to himself, working out the key moment to cash in.

Morgrave jerked Martha back into the room, sneering, "Don't worry your little head, Elizabeth Montgomery. I'll take good care of her." He slammed the door, leaving Beth in the dark, her daughter's last word echoing in her ears.

Outside of town, Edgar was running to the Wampanoag camp faster than he'd ever run in his life— what else could he do?

— Chapter 15 —

Breathless and near collapse, Edgar ran to the center of the Wampanoag camp and screamed as loud as he could, "PASHANOK! PASHANOK! HELP! HELP!"

It came out as a loud croak, but it was enough to alarm all those at the gathering fire. Pashanok ran to him, took a knee and grabbed him by the shoulders.

Before he could ask, Edgar blurted out, "Morgrave! Beth!and Martha! The ship! The ship!" and began to shake and wail.

Pashanok lifted the boy's chin gently and got his attention, "Tell me more, Edgar. I will help, but I need to know everything. Can you do that?"

He nodded, gulped, and took a deep breath.

"That Lord! Morgrave! He took Beth on the ship. In chains. Reverend Mayhew couldn't save her. It sails tonight. Martha tried to save her. I helped. But—" He began to whimper.

"But—go on, Edgar. Go on—I'm listening."

"But Martha was caught too! And I just, I just ran away!" He began to cry again even louder.

Pashanok felt the boy's regret and the pain of his

conscience. Edgar didn't comprehend how brave he'd been in so many ways—up against adults fighting for a girl and her mother.

"Did you see the ship leave the harbor? Do you know where it's headed?"

Edgar thought long and hard. "It was still in the harbor when I left, but she was ready to make way on the next tide. A sailor told me so."

"Where was it headed?" Pashanok urged him to remember if he knew at all.

"I—I never heard." Edgar slumped to the ground, fully spent.

"That's okay. You've given me a chance to save them."

The last line was cast from the dock and the ship was under way. Beth was alerted to the subtle sway of the current as it pulled her and Martha away from their home, away from the cottage, Argon—Pashanok!

She heaved a heavy sigh, fighting hopeless resignation. She thought to herself, We must never give in. Never. She heard Martha crying through the thin paneled closet door where she was imprisoned.

"Martha!" She said firmly.

The crying stopped.

"Mom?" Came the reply. "I'm so sorry Mother. I tried—but"

She started to cry again.

"Martha!" Beth repeated out loud what she'd told herself, "We must never give in. Never!"

Martha tried to wriggle free from the chair she was tied to, her feet to the legs, her hands behind her back. She worked her hands back and forth with no results.

They both heard Morgrave's footsteps across the deck, his boots distinctly different from the sailor's bare feet. He stomped twice outside the door for effect, then swept the door open as if to discover some newly imagined escape plot. He paused outside Beth's door, then strode over to Martha with a sweeping dramatic flourish, impressing himself with smug satisfaction. Lord Morgrave slammed his fist on the table; a pewter mug fell to the floor.

Beth heard Martha squeal in fear.

Pashanok ran to the cliffs overlooking the harbor. Among the forest of masts in the silvery moonlight there were just a few moving on the tide. Only one set belonged to a ship the size he was looking for. He tracked it carefully until the heavy black shadow of its hull turned east off the northern tip of **Cheppiaquidne**.

He gathered the longest coil of rope he could find and a deer's antler he'd shaped into a large hook. As he ran south along the cliff path, he remembered a poem from long ago, one that summoned the spirits of the sea and the sky. He drew on everything he knew and felt, sensing the energy flowing through his body with every breath, every step. Then he began to chant—low at first, a vibration in his chest, calling to those who had heard his ancestors for generations.

Kehutamuwô wutahkomuk,
Nôpaheesu nashpe kesuk
Nôpaheesu nashpe tôk
Kehutamuwô kehkitôk,
Neesqutôtam nashpe papôut.

Hear me, great ocean,
Bright sun in the sky,
I rise from the deep,
Hear me, great wind,
Stand with me in the storm.

The moon lit his path in the sandy soil like a glowing thread snaking into the distance. He made it to the beach in good time, surprised he didn't feel tired at all. Quite the opposite, he felt invigorated; even more alive. He took a knee and felt the cool sand pour through his fingers watching for the wind direction. Good. It was flowing with the current to the east.

The ship had to turn west into the wind and current, slowing it's progress. If he could get into that current and intercept the ship? In that moment, he saw a long shadow in the dunes covered in seaweed. It was an old dugout **moashoon** that had washed ashore during a summer storm long ago. Was this a gift from Keesoq to help him succeed?

Martha swore to herself and all that's good in the world, she would fight to the very end. When Morgrave dared to whisper in her ear about all the things he would do to her, she turned quickly and bit down hard on his ear, almost severing half of it from his head. He bellowed like a wounded animal and shrieked obscenities as he clutched the fragments of his ear, blood spilling between his fingers.

Beth heard the high pitched screaming and wailing through the wall and thought it was Martha at first. Then, miraculously, as Morgrave stood back and took a short breath, she heard Martha laugh maliciously.

"You will learn, little bird!" Morgrave roared with fire in his eyes, 'Never dare to taunt the Devil himself!"

Beth heard the loudest slap, Martha's grunt, and the sound of her chair hit the deck as Martha landed with a crash.

"Leave her alone, you coward!" Beth screamed at the top of her lungs.

Morgrave kicked Martha in the back, but the chair took the worst of it. "You're next, Mother dear!" He said loudly in a sweet mocking manner.

Pashanok uncovered the stench of rotten crabs and fish when he swept seaweed from the old canoe. That would wash away quickly enough. He dragged it down to the water and readied himself for his mission. He pulled the coil of rope off his shoulder and tied one end around his waist so it wouldn't slip off, and tied the antler hook to the other end.

He closed his eyes and imagined the ocean spirit carrying him on a giant pôhtam in the current as the hungry **shokan** let him go by. He saw the ship trying to avoid him by tacking side to side, but they couldn't escape. No . . . his combined energy with Elizabeth and Martha would not be denied.

With a smile and a deep breath, he hauled the canoe into the water and shoved it before him into the surf. With a gurgling hiss it abruptly took on water and sank directly to the bottom. His heart sank with it for a moment. But then he thought, this is not an omen for me. This was the boat's destiny, not mine. I will take this as a good sign.

Now more confident than ever, Pashanok charged into the shore-break and dove deep, riding the under-tow as long as he could. He felt the extra weight of the rope fighting his ascent to the surface. The warrior broke free a great distance from shore.

He felt the tidal current pull him along and just remembered seeing a friend of his youth lost to the sea in the same way. A twinge of fear poked at his heart. This would be like threading a needle while racing by on horseback! He could not lose hope. He would not lose hope. His life would not be worth living without Elizabeth and Martha in it!

He scanned the horizon for a ship's moonlit sails. After a time he saw what looked like a small low cloud on the horizon to the east. It didn't behave like a cloud though. It had to be the ship. His heart sank as it slid farther and farther south and away from him, but then it tacked back to the north!

Captain Drake heard Morgrave's loud cursing and the young women protesting from his state room. Then the crash of the chair. Beth screaming. The poor girl! His chivalrous young officers looked to him for direction. Would he allow this abuse to continue? Was he condoning the torture of women aboard his ship?

He heard a rap on his cabin door. "Enter." He responded.

The First Mate stepped in and saluted, "Captain, Sir. There have been reports of a disturbance from a few of the men. It seems our passengers have been in some kind of conflict, sir." He said with the utmost of diplomacy. "Shall I go and question them on the matter?"

A loud shout came from Morgrave, then his door slammed. The sound of his boots stomping down the deck ended when he stepped down the ladder to a deck further below.

"No Stanley, I'll take care of this." The Captain shook his head. "I've had enough of this Lord Morgrave and his tyranny. It's time he understood this ship is under my command!"

The two of them stepped out the door and stopped short. There was a trail of blood drops leading away from Morgrave's door.

The Captain threw open the door to Margrave's cabin. He rushed over to Martha when he saw she was spitting blood and wriggling against the ropes around her feet and hands. She had already freed one foot from the splintered chair leg, and it was only a matter of time before her hands were free.

Drake tipped the chair and Martha back upright.

"'He was going to kill me! Or worse!" Martha declared with judicial force. "He must be arrested and put in chains at once!"

"I will see to Morgrave just as soon as I can." He assured her, "Right now, let's tend to you."

"You have to help my mother!" Martha pleaded. "He'll do the same to her! He promised he would!"

"Now that is a different matter." He looked up as he untied her other foot, "Lord Morgrave has authority over your mother's imprisonment and I must stand on the law."

"But sir—" Martha protested, "If the King knew—"

"No. There can be no dispute on this." He untied her hands from the chair but kept them bound behind her. "Until you respect the law and my authority on this ship, you must be held in my quarters."

"Captain! Sir!" The First Mate ran in from the main deck, "You're needed on deck!"

Drake felt an uneasy shiver as the ship quaked and shimmied. "Take her to my cabin, then report to the helm!"

Pashanok swam with the current and the wind, feeling the ocean pull him along like a river and just as fast. Before long, he could see the dark rigging against the moonlit sails, each mast and spar against the sky, and tiny yellow lights like fireflies blinking in the breeze. He felt like one of those little water bugs floating on the surface.

As the ship approached it began to turn away again, making it's tack to the south. Only a short distance separated them, but it may as well have been miles because it—and Beth and Martha—were slowly getting farther and farther away. Then he realized—the ship hadn't tacked. Something was pushing it away. But then it came closer. He looked more closely and saw the surface swirling, tossing and glowing!

There were no waves but the sea was jumping along a line from the island out into the ocean. Pashanok felt himself being sucked into a jumble of swirling currents moving in every direction. Some pushed him up, but the worst pulled him down. The new waters were frigid and his teeth began chattering. He grit his teeth and tried to swim to the ship, but there was nothing he could do.

At the helm aboard the ship, the Captain called to the First Mate, "Rudder hard to port! We're floundering in confused waters where two currents grind against each other! Keep our tack to the north!" The First Mate turned to the Navigator who warned that these waters frequently created shallows north towards the island.

"We can't hold this heading for much longer Captain!" he replied.

A call came from the stern where the Second Mate held a sounding line to test depth, "By the mark, four. sir!"

A few minutes later with urgency, "By the mark, three! Sir!"

The First Mate called out "By Jove, hard to lee! Come about! Bear off this heading!"

The helmsman spun the wheel as fast as he could to starboard now, and the ship stalled as the crew worked the sails to the new heading.

In the water below, Pashanok realized his time had come. The ocean spirit delivered the ship to him, and now he had to act. He was being tossed about while it stalled in the current, but he calmed his nerves. took his antler hook and heaved it at the side of the ship.

It clattered and fell to the water.

He hauled it in and gave it another heave. It hooked onto a porthole for a moment, then slipped as he pulled it tighter.

He swung it over his head, and just as he threw it a wave tossed him up in the air. The hook snagged on the rigging at the rail and held fast.

As the ship began to make way Pashanok had a new problem. The hull was covered in a crust of sharp-edged barnacles ready to shred his skin to a pulp. He unraveled the rope as fast as he could and bobbed along in the wake, relieved the first stage of his plan had worked—mostly.

—*Chapter 16*—

Edgar trudged along the wooded path, guilt pressing on his chest like a millstone. Pashanok had refused his help, choosing instead to slip into the night alone—determined to save Beth and Martha by his own hand. Edgar had told himself it was for the best, that he would only slow the warrior down, but the words rang hollow.

Argon's bark split the night air as the cottage came into view. Of course—the animals. He had almost forgotten. Life, in its stubborn way, still demanded its ordinary duties even when the world felt as though it were coming apart.

Inside, the small home smelled faintly of salt air and Martha's wildflowers. A single beach rose blossom lay on her bed—faded now, but still holding the ghost of its fragrance. Edgar stood staring at it, the soft petals a sharp reminder of how quickly things had changed. Only days ago, Martha had been a bright, untouchable force in his world; now, she was somewhere in the grip of a man capable of anything. He felt the shift in himself then—a quiet, hardening resolve. Whatever happened, he would not stand idle again.

Argon whined from the doorway, snapping him back.

Edgar fetched the dinner bowl and banged it twice, and the dog came running, tail thrashing. After the goats were settled and the hens quieted, Edgar lowered himself into Beth's worn chair by the front door. As he leaned back, he thought he saw a flicker of movement beyond the window—a shadow gliding past the tree line—but when he turned his head, there was only the restless sway of branches in the moonlight.

The wood creaked beneath him, the night wind whispering through the shutters. Exhaustion tugged at him until he could no longer resist, and he drifted into uneasy dreams, Argon curled warm against his boots.

Pashanok kept hold of his rope, dragging behind the ship like bait at the end of a line. The chill of the water was beginning to wear him down, his feet were going numb and he switched his lead hand out back and forth as the grip of his wounded arm began to falter.

A sailor at the stern rail was still lowering a knotted rope into the water intermittently, then calling something out to someone Pashanok couldn't see. The rope was tightly secured to the rail, certainly more secure than his rope and hook set-up was.

The churning wake turbulence spun Pashanok back and forth as he started to haul himself in closer to the ship. He refused to acknowledge the complaints coming from his exhausted body. The closer he got to the ship's rudder, the closer he was to the sailor's rope. The sailor had been coming and going at regular intervals, but he had been gone for awhile now, and unlike the previous times he had left the rope dangling over the side.

Pashanok used his body like a rudder, angled against the wake current and slid sideways up to the rope. He held there for a moment when the extra force against the barnacle-crusted hull caused his own rope's chafed strands to snap one by one until it parted with a sharp crack! Pashanok dropped back into the surge, the cold closing over his head. For a heartbeat the current tried to claim him, dragging him into the dark. He kicked hard, breaking surface, teeth bared against the salt.

Above him, another line still dangled from the stern: the sounding rope left by the second mate. With a desperate lunge he grabbed the sailors knotted rope with his bleeding hand, and wrapped it twice around his wrist. He heaved a sigh of relief, despite the pain shooting through his wounded arm, hot and merciless. Pashanok now clung desperately to his only hope, knowing much more than his own life hung in the void. Just then, he looked up and made direct eye contact with the second mate who had returned to the rail.

The man screamed in surprise and ran away yelling, "Mermaid! Uh—Mer-man! On the sounding line! Mer-man! Captain! CAPTAIN!"

Pashanok refused to be caught on a line like some namohs!

Hand over hand he climbed, slamming against the hull where barnacles tore new cuts across his chest and legs; the salt forcing every scrape to burn like fire. He found the right moment, gripped the ornate transom and moved like an animal, pulling himself up the slick timbers, his limbs spread wide.

The second mate returned to the rail with the few others willing to entertain his little fantasy. They jeered at him when the sounding line came up empty, and laughed even harder at his protestations. To any eye above, he was only another shadow shifting against the ship's carved stern.

At last his fingers found the carved cornice below the captain's gallery. He hooked himself there, clinging with quiet tenacity, his body flattened against the wood. Each breath was shallow, measured, as the water dripped from his hair and the ship creaked around him.

The wound in his forearm pulsed, the blood smearing across the carving. But his eyes were clear, fixed above. Elizabeth. Martha. They were here. And no pain, no tide, no English steel would keep him from them now. I will be a **m'suhtam** tonight! he smiled to himself.

Morgrave found Skip grumbling in the galley corner as he peeled potatoes while the cook hacked away at a gamey looking piece of mutton. The boy dropped what he was doing as soon as he saw blood on his master's shoulder, dripping from the side of his head.

Morgrave had no time for sentiment. He yelled at the cook, "Put that aside, ye useless kettle warmer! Get over here and tend to my ear!"

The heavy-set cook wiped the cleaver on his dirty

apron and sucked the meat juice off his sausage-like fingers.

"Right!" He replied with a wink to Skip, "The shark asking the manatee for a patch-up I see."

Morgrave relaxed his hand slightly.

Skip's stomach heaved at the sight of Morgrave's mangled ear.

"Just get to it!" Morgrave demanded.

The cook took a box from the spice shelf above the stove, blew the dust off it and rummaged for a needle and waxed thread.

He turned to Skip, "Run to your master's quarters and fetch his rum. We'll be needing that too."

Skip was eager to oblige.

Beth listened intently for anything that might tell her how Martha was doing. She heard Morgrave shout, slam the door and march off down the deck. She heard the Captain and First Mate talking about Morgrave, muffled voices as they came and went. She called Martha's name and heard nothing. She worried. Her heart ached to know what happened. Some time had passed and her concern kept building, yet she was helpless to act.

Now in the Captain's stateroom, Martha was set on getting free. Once he was gone, she used her teeth on the ropes binding her wrists, grunting and moaning with effort. She just had to rescue her mother. But how could they hide on the ship when so many would be looking for them? It was guaranteed suicide to jump overboard, but she would do it with her mom if all else failed.

One thing at a time, she thought. First, she had to break free.

Captain Drake appreciated the crew's high spirits, joking about the Second Mate's "Mer-man sighting" and joined in by insisting he record it in the ship's log. Within minutes he had forgotten about the drama below-decks with Morgrave and his bizarre appetite for causing pain. The confused waters and island currents were behind them and soon they'd be on a direct westerly course for New Amsterdam. He patted the First Mate on the back, gave him the helm and was about to descend to the main deck when a call came from the crow's nest high on the main mast.

"Storm clouds brewing off the port bow!" The sailor repeated the call a few times.

The Captain returned to the helm. "What do you think, Stanley?"

They both watched the horizon intently. Lightning flickered in the distance.

"Change our bearing to the northwest." He said "Storm like that will sweep us up before we know it."

"I agree." Drake nodded and jabbed a thumb over his shoulder. "We've already had enough bad luck with those two skirted jinxes."

He looked up at the sails in the cool blue moonlight

and headed to his cabin.

Edgar was jolted awake by a poke to his shoulder. He looked up, wide eyed, to see Tobiasquam standing there in the moonlight with his arms folded.

"Where are Martha and Beth?" He asked. "They aren't with the tribe—and my uncle is gone too."

Argon was standing next to him with the same quizzical look.

Edgar wiped the sleep from his eyes, "You don't know?"

"Know what?" He was immediately alarmed. "Where are they!"

Edgar explained everything as best he could from what happened at the church to his and Martha's failed rescue and finally Pashanok's own mission that he didn't know much about. Tobiasquam glared at Edgar for not inviting him to help and felt a little offended.

To his credit, Edgar picked up on that and said, "It happened so fast! We were just caught up in it all."

"Wampanuit sent me to find you." The young Wampanoag was very serious, "You have to come back to Katama."

Skip hesitated outside Morgrave's door and thought of smacking Martha around himself while Beth was forced to watch. But then he remembered Morgrave's wrath and had an idea. The Captain was up on deck dealing with sailor stuff. Why not dip into his rum supply instead of Morgraves?

He twisted the knob quietly and edged the Captain's door open cautiously. Then he slowly stuck his head inside, hoping no one was there. WHACK! Martha struck the back of his head as hard as she could with the butt of the captain's musket. Skip fell to the floor, out cold. For a moment she just stood over him, chest heaving, the musket still heavy in her hands. Skip's sprawled form looked smaller than she remembered, not the sly tormentor who had mocked her mother but just a boy, foolish and cruel. Her hands trembled, but it wasn't fear anymore—it was something stronger, steadier. For once, she wasn't the hunted child. She was the one who struck first.

Martha edged out the door and hid behind a line of crates just as the Captain came into view.

Pashanok felt the ship turn before most of the sailors did. He had been searching his perch for a way to climb higher up to the rail, but the overhang was too great and he couldn't risk falling off. As the ship turned north, the southern horizon swung into view along with the moonlit storm clouds. Lightning flickered reflections on the water. Now he knew why they had turned back towards the coast.

A light shone through the windows above.

He grasped part of the decorative cornice and stood to peer inside. The scene within so shocked him with surprise; he nearly fell from the ship!

The Captain stood in the cabin doorway with a musket in one hand and a dazed young teen boy in the other, looking around with the fires of hell in his eyes. He dragged the boy over to a table covered with charts and scrolls, dumped him in a chair and slung the gun on the wall.

"That does it!" He slammed his fist on the table, "By Jove, this infernal Morgrave treachery ends NOW! Breaking into my quarters! Setting a prisoner free! Pilfering my musket! You'll get a few stripes for this you scupper-brained sea whelp!"

The petrified street urchin found his moment and dashed out the door and down the ladder between decks in two giant steps. He raced to Morgrave's room and locked himself inside.

The Captain followed in hot pursuit.

Pashanok watched with the spirit of a **pussoúgh**, ready to spring when the moment arrived. He reached over and felt the window frame for an opening and to his surprise it slid sideways towards him! Without a second thought, he climbed into the room, landed softly and hid under the table.

Now to find Beth and Môsi.

Martha heard the Captain's voice as he left the helm above, dropped the musket and padded back down to Morgrave's room.

"Mom? Are you in here?" She called out in a loud whisper, "Where are you?"

"I'm here! In the closet!" came Beth's muffled reply from behind a door across the room.

Martha threw open the door to reveal her mother seated on the floor chained the ship's timber frame.

The tears flowed freely as she embraced her mother.

"Let me look at you!" Beth asked and Martha stood back, "Your eye!"

Martha's eye was already turning shades of purple from Morgrave's backhanded blow, but she was more concerned about the bloodied shackles holding Beth captive.

She stepped forward to examine the manacles, looking for a way to open them.

"Morgrave locked them with a key he keeps in his vest pocket." Beth explained. "Somehow we have to get it. But Martha—"

"I know Mom. Please trust me. I can do this. I will not fail this time."

'No Martha. Please don't. He'll capture—" But Martha was already opening the door intent on gaining the upper hand.

"I can do this Mom."

"God be with you! I will pray—". Exhausted, Beth slumped to the floor, already filled with new anxieties.

Martha sneaked out the door, then ducked behind a water barrel lashed to the inner hull as Skip came flying down the ladder. He ran to Morgrave's door and locked himself inside. She attempted to leave, but then the captain followed, grumbling and cursing.

Wampanuit sat the boys down on a log near the glowing embers of the dying communal fire. He stood before them more serious than Tobiasquash had ever seen. Edgar was both petrified and in awe of this clear eyed older man and the tribal camp around him. Wampanuit made sweeping gestures and spoke in a melodic language he recognized, but didn't understand.

Tobiasquash translated, "A great storm is here. We must go to Aquinnah."

Edgar looked up quizzically at the cloudless, starry sky.

Wampanuit spoke again, more insistently.

Edgar heard names.

"Pashanok will be there." Tobiasquam said. "And Beth and Môsi."

"Wait—Who? Where?" Edgar protested. "I don't understand. Who is Môsi?"

Tobiasquam put his hand up.

Wampanuit cupped his hands to his mouth and made a call Tobiasquash had never heard before. To Edgar's astonishment, his horse appeared from behind a wigwam.

Within minutes they were galloping off together into the night, holding on for dear life—

— *Chapter 17* —

Pashanok had never been inside a ship before. He had always watched from the shore as they drifted past the island on the wind; sometimes fast, sometimes barely moving. He took a look at his surroundings from beneath the table. The captain's state room was unlike any he'd been in before. It had gentle curves in the ceiling and walls with beams everywhere. There were fancy flags, decorations, and different kinds of weapons displayed here and there. More importantly, there was no place to hide except for where he was, and that wasn't too good either.

He heard the captain one deck below, banging on something while yelling a steady stream of threats and curses. Pashanok looked around again. He spied a hat on a hook near the door, and the captain's coat on the chair nearby, then a pair of britches on a drying rack by a cabinet with drawers. What if—he thought—

The storm winds had picked up dramatically, taking the First Mate and crew by surprise. The ship was beginning to lean and groan with too much sail aloft for the weather. The rigging began to whistle in the gale force winds as a loose line whipped around dangerously before being caught and tied down. The sea was starting to roll, breakers gaining in size by the minute. They were still on the northwesterly course, tacking away from the storm, but somehow it seemed to have singled them out and was chasing them down.

"Damn those blasted she-witches Morgrave brought on board!" A grizzled old sailor muttered to himself, "They be the death of us all!"

The First Mate sent a sailor to fetch the Captain and ordered others up into the rigging to hoist in the topmost sails before they pulled part of a mast down. They clamored up the ratlines clinging to the shrouds like insects running up a branch in the wind. The storm-driven sea threw barrels of water against them from the waves below, every cold drop stinging like the cat-o-nine-tails.

The cook looked at Morgrave who was sitting on a stool, leaning against the wall waiting for Skip to return. He held his fragmented ear against his head, the blood flow had diminished some.

"We better get on with the sewing there, sir." The cook advised as he threaded a long, curved needle with waxed black thread, "If that starts drying up on it's own there'll be no blood to glue it together."

"If that's your expert opinion, cookie." Morgrave grumbled sarcastically.

"It is, in fact." The cook turned surgeon nodded. "I served in His Majesty's Navy for a month of years and seen every kind of wound possible, and some looked impossible." He gave a good guffaw at his own joke.

"Just do it or I'll have to do it myself!" Morgrave was seething.

"You'll have to sit still now." The cook ignored his comment leaned on him with his greasy belly and apron. "Let go of that ear now."

The ship hit a wave just as the cook inserted his needle into the remaining part of Lord Morgrave's ear, sending the two of them tumbling in different directions. The severed portion was lost in the dirt and dust under the stove, while Morgrave himself slammed into the chopping block covered in mutton chops. The cook, ever used to rough seas below-decks, caught himself with one hand on a ceiling beam and the other on the doorjamb.

The bucking continued and Morgrave fell to the floor, angry as an injured wolf. He leapt to his feet and stuck his finger in the cook's face, "I'll have you swinging from the yard-arm after you're keel hauled, you brainless bilge rat!"

The cook grabbed his cleaver and raised it in response while another wave pitched Morgrave backwards into the spice shelf. He turned and scrambled out the door as the cook shrugged and got back to work. A bilge rat scampered back into the pantry locker with Morgrave's severed ear in his teeth.

Beth was tossed back and forth in the closet until she braced her legs against the wall and door. She heard footsteps rush in, the door slam, and a chair scrape across the floor.

"Martha? Is that you?" she asked, hope breaking through her voice.

Skip gave a nasty little chuckle as he jammed the chair against the knob. "No mommy. She's busy now. Your daughter has much to learn."

Beth's blood went cold.

Skip spat on the floor near the door and laughed scornfully now. "Don't worry, Witch. She'll keep uncle Goodwin entertained long enough. And me? I'll make sure she never forgets the name 'Skip Frey'."

He kicked the chair hard to wedge it tighter against the outer door, leaving Beth trembling in the dark—the chains cutting deeper—not into her wrists, but her heart.

When the Captain arrived and started battering the door with his fists, Skip saw that it wouldn't budge and yelled back, "Lord Morgrave will have your head for treating royal guests like this, you louse infested gutter pig!"

Drake went apoplectic with rage, "This door will come down, and you'll be shark fodder before the day is done! My oath to God Himself!"

Beth took the opportunity and screamed for help, adding her plight to Skip's woes.

Morgrave stumbled up the deck from midships, holding on for dear life as the waves continued to build. Seawater came down the gangways in waterfalls from the deck above, splashing about his knees before spilling out the scuppers. He'd forgotten about his ear for the moment.

Martha heard him cursing as he made his way toward his cabin. She hid deeper behind the water barrels, pressing her back into the damp wood, heart thudding, hoping she'd find her moment to act.

Then the air shifted around her. The creak of the ship's timbers grew faint, replaced by a hush like wind through tall reeds. A shimmer opened at her side, and for a moment she was no longer crouched in the shadows but standing barefoot in a different place. Beside her crouched the beautiful woman from her earlier vision—but she was much younger now—hair tangled, wearing a poor farmer's britches. The young woman clutched her hand as if they were one in danger together. The words "I'm sorry, mother" softly echoed through Martha's mind, stunning her somehow with unknown regret.

Martha blinked, and the barrels returned. The smell of tar and salt rushed back into her lungs. Her hand was empty, yet it still tingled with the warmth of that grasp. She swallowed hard, knowing she carried not just her own courage, but her mother's as well.

When Morgrave saw Captain Drake cursing and beating on his state room door, he screamed, "What the Devil are you doing, you scurvy half-wit! Get away from there at once! In the name of the Crown!"

The First Mate came part way down the gangway, battling the deluge of seawater and yelled to the Captain, "Sir, we need you topsides at the helm, Sir! She aims to flounder on the shallows if we don't ease her up soon!"

"I will deal with you and your little scalawag later, Morgrave!" Drake stormed by shaking his fist. He climbed up the ladder like he had his entire life and was gone to save the ship.

"Skipper my boy! Good job holding back that good-for-nothing blow hard!" Morgrave said through the door in his cheeriest voice, "We can celebrate with that rum you were fetching for your Uncle Goodwin!"

Beth recognized Morgrave's voice and felt an uncontrollable shiver run up her spine. Her stomach tensed as she heard Skip hesitantly pull the chair from the door. More concerning than that, where was Martha? What could she be doing?

Morgrave entered like a ferocious beast, growling every word from clenched teeth. "I'll rip you limb from limb, boy! My ear is permanently destroyed you lollygagging wastrel! You had one job! Get my rum for me! But here you are, setting the girl free!"

He rocked with every wave, teetering like a drunk on a bender. Skip danced back and forth, avoiding debris awash on the floor while hoping to find a means to flee again. Beth held tight, she truly prayed the two would find a way to kill each other.

Skip swore his unconditional loyalty to Morgrave, pleading for a chance of redemption. He steadied himself against a cabinet by the door that held rum and wine, the battered door swung open and closed.

"Here Uncle Goodwin!" He grasped a bottle behind him and held it out plaintively, "We can toast your victory!" he squeaked, his voice cracking like the child he was.

The bottle trembled in his hand, sloshing against the neck as he thrust it toward Morgrave like a peace offering, like a shield.

"Give me that!" Morgrave lunged at him, eyes wild with anger, blood staining his neck and collar.

The boy jumped in fear; the bottle flipped in the air. Morgrave snatched it with the speed of a snake.

"Go drown, for all I care." His voice dripping with venom.

Skip bolted, slipping on the wet planks, his cry for help swallowed by the storm. Lightning lit him in flashes as he skittered past Marthanot a villain now, not even a rival, only a boy fleeing into a night that had no use for him. But boys like Skip had a way of surviving when better souls could not.

Her gut feeling was to stay put.

Captain Drake stood braced at the helm, the First Mate at the wheel, the Second Mate shouting orders through a speaking trumpet to the crew; some in the rigging, others on deck.

The storm had caught them.

Lightning flashed all around, each bolt threatening to poke a hole through the ship and sink her directly. An endless river of water flowed from port to starboard carrying random things yanked from their lashings. A few fish flapped helplessly on deck then were carried back overboard. Sailors grappled with sails cracking in the wind along-side thunderclaps just a bit louder.

Then, amidst all the tumult and sea-sawing insanity, the ship suddenly stabilized as if it were a living thing. The entire crew was awestruck by the phenomenon. At first,

Drake thought they'd run aground on a sandbar, but there was no sickening grind or the sound of splintering wood. Just the opposite, it felt like the ship was rising from the water, as if riding the back of a whale or some otherworldly sea monster!

Pashanok saw the seas rising and felt the storm surging towards the ship even as the crew frantically scurried about to save their souls. He knew better from the start. Whether they lived or died depended less on their wisdom and skill than if the sea spirits allowed them to. Some ships survived. Others didn't. His mission was to find Beth and Martha, then by those same spirits somehow deliver them all to shore.

He slipped into the britches as he'd seen men do, then a tunic, then the coat. He pulled a sword from the wall and strapped it to his waist. Finally, he donned the hat and by chance noticed his reflection in a polished metal plaque on the wall. He was no **maneechuwô** or **chôkannês**, but his disguise would have to do. He looked down at the captain's boots and shook his head, now that's going too far, he thought.

Pashanok left the captain's quarters just as the ship began to stabilize. He felt an energy through his feet, up his legs and into his gut. The storm outside was fierce as ever, but the ship itself was calm somehow. Just then the Second Mate came down the gangway behind him,

"Captain!" He saluted reflexively, despite having just seen Drake at the helm, then looked down quizzically and saw Pashanok's bare feet. The tribesman turned around and the sailor screamed, running back up the gangway three rungs at a time, "The—the—Mer-man! He's—He's Mer'man! MERMAN!"

Pashanok shrugged and shook his head, then using the calm within the ship, listened intently for anything that might alert him to Beth or Martha.

Then he heard something strangely familiar. It was the voice he'd heard in the forest. The man who had his locket. The one with the dagger. And that boy! They were close, and that meant Beth and Martha must also be nearby! He crouched instinctively and padded across the deck like a cat to the next gangway.

The voices got louder.

They were arguing in a room down below. The door had been banging open and close, but now it was open. He peered down to see the boy running away, the chôkânuwô yelled after him, "When I catch you, there'll be hell to pay!".

The human predator sensed Pashanok looking down but wasn't quick enough to catch him.

The Second Mate came running up to the Captain and First Mate with his crazy "Mer-man" nonsense again, claiming this time he was below-decks and wearing a captain's uniform! As the First Mate held his stomach in laughter, Drake felt some trepidation setting in. The ship's strange behavior still had no explanation, and they were now higher off the water and actually moving impossibly FASTER!

He could see the breakers crashing against

Tequenoman off the port bow and the cliffs of Aquinnah were coming into view off the starboard bow! The ship seemed as if to be in the grip of something like a giant hand!

The storm was still beating at the sails while lightning flashed all around, and thunder kept his ears ringing and his heart pounding. He spun the wheel hard in either direction but it did no good. He had no control at all! Just then, a blood curdling scream came from high above in the crow's nest. The lookout sailor was pointing behind them to the south.

He turned back just as another lightning bolt flashed and the First Mate's eyes flew wide open, his body stiff as a corpse. Drake spun again, and this time the next flash split the sky like rivers of fire.

For an instant—no longer than the breath between thunder—a giant Wampanoag warrior seemed to stand in the sea behind them, as tall as the ship was long. The form waded through the churning water, one vast arm sweeping at its side, the other appearing to rise beneath the hull itself, as if the ship were being held up by the storm's own will.

His face was set like stone in purpose, his fierce eyes seemed to capture the lightning itself. Rain and surf streaked across his glistening skin, yet the water never seemed to cling, sliding away through his body as if he was the storm itself and his breath, the wind.

Then the thunder collapsed upon itself, the light shattered, and the sea was only sea again—raging, blind, and empty—leaving Drake unsure whether he had witnessed a thing that stood in the world, or the world briefly remembering something older than sight.

The Second Mate lost his mind in a panic, jumped overboard and was lost to the churning currents. Other sailors ran for the lifeboat davits, fumbling desperately trying to work the winches. With each stride, the giant was moving them faster towards the waters off Aquinnah.

Another bolt of lightning came down, striking the center mast then running down through the hull into the sea below leaving the scent of burning tar behind. Waves continued to crash and thunder, but the giant was not deterred.

Pashanok watched Morgrave slink back into his cabin, now more confident on the stabilized deck. He quietly stepped down the ladder to the deck below, then took off the Captain's hat and slipped out of the coat.

Martha gasped with joy and almost squealed his name! She couldn't help herself!

Pashanok snapped around and gestured for her to be quiet. He couldn't hold back a smile at seeing her too. But now it was time to deal with Morgrave.

He crept to the door crab-walking below eye level. This time he knew what to expect from this enemy. There would be no surprises. He had everything on his side, and a sword. He slowly turned the doorknob and edged the door open, then he leapt into the room, ready for a fight. But Morgrave had vanished somehow! He was gone!

Truth be told, Morgrave had heard Martha's gasp.

Pashanok was dumbfounded. He began to look, frantically at first—then more carefully. Was there a secret passageway? Did he sneak out the transom window somehow? No. Where was Beth? He turned and looked back toward Martha who was pointing at a door across the room. A closet that blended in with the wall paneling.

He heard the faintest movement inside and positioned himself so the door would shield him. When he snapped it open, Morgrave lunged into the room, dagger flashing, certain this time he would reach Martha.

The blade met only air.

Morgrave recoiled. Pashanok stepped fully into view, the sword's tip leveled at his chest. Beth cried out as Morgrave seized her and dragged the dagger to her throat, the metal dimpling her skin.

"Back away, savage," Morgrave hissed. "Drop the sword or I'll cut her."

A thin line of blood appeared at Beth's neck.

"Run him through, Pasha!" she screamed.

"Drop it. Now."

Pashanok saw the truth of it in Morgrave's eyes—the man would kill her whether he obeyed or not. And he knew, with a certainty that burned, that Martha would never forgive him if Beth died. Nor would he.

The sword began to lower.

"No!—Mom!"

Martha burst across the room and hurled herself at Morgrave with all her weight.

The dagger slashed wildly, but Pashanok surged forward and drove the captain's sword through Morgrave's arm, pinning it to the beam. Morgrave shrieked as the blade fell from his hand.

Beth twisted, looping the chains binding her wrists around Morgrave's neck. She braced her feet and pulled hard until he sagged forward, choking. His body went slack—left hanging by the skewered arm alone.

Martha tore at Morgrave's vest until she found the key and freed the irons. Mother and daughter clung to one another, shaking, breathless.

"What is it, Pasha?" Beth asked.

Pashanok stood frozen at the porthole, staring into the storm-dark sea.

"Moshup," he said.

The top deck was complete chaos. Sailors were running about screaming as the ship was shoved onto the

Devil's Bridge, a shallow ridge that runs like a granite spine off the coast of Aquinnah. It shuddered to a complete stop in the midst of splintered beams and broken masts, the sails fell like a death shroud over the doomed ship.

Captain Drake was thrown into the wheel as it spun uncontrollably, his body broken in seconds. The First Mate fell to the main deck where a wave swept him into the churning sea. Sailors and passengers alike were caught in the maelstrom, some clinging to life longer than others, before the storm decided..

Morgrave woke bound by his own irons, chained to the beam where Beth had been. The water was already at his chest, and rising.

Pashanok staring out the window, transfixed, while Beth and Martha were pleading for him to go. But go where? There was no escape—not yet.

He felt a heavy breath outside and turned. Martha felt it too. Each listened—not to the waves or the thunder, but something that moved beneath it all. The gale-torn sails strained like a giant against the storm. Below them, the ship screamed as fingers of jagged stone tore into its belly.. Rushing waters flowed like blood, surging through open gashes in the hull.

As the water closed around his throat, Morgrave pleaded for his life. He offered wealth and power, then cursed them with every threat he could summon. He raged like a beast, then sobbed like a child—but they heard none of it.

Mercy was not for them to give. If Moshup saved him then so be it.

"There is one thing you will surrender to me," Pashanok said. He dug into the folds of Morgrave's torn vest as he struggled and retrieved the locket. He forced Morgrave to look—Elizabeth's portrait smiled sweetly in the dim moonlight.

"She is free of you," Pashanok said. "For all time."

A wave came from the south as if guided by a large hand. It crashed through the transom, and swept them into the sea.

As they were spinning and twisting in the turbulence, a lifeboat fell from a shattered davit nearly hitting Pashanok when it landed. He caught hold of the bowline, tipped the boat to the side and helped Beth in.

He turned again—

Martha was gone.

Pashanok led the boat as he swam, while Beth searched the wild currents around them. They found boards and beams and drifting barrels—but still, no Martha.

The storm broke as quickly as it had come. Wind fell away. The sea loosened its grip. Dawn crept in as the tide carried them toward Aquinnah, pale light chasing the last stars from the sky.

At last, Pashanok pulled himself into the boat. They clung to one another and wept—bitter, wordless grief for their Môsi, the love of their lives. The surf thundered against the shore, growing louder with every breath.

They paddled with their hands toward land, the storm still echoing in their bones, calling her name again and again—

"MARTHA!"

"MÔSI!"

Until their voices broke too.

Elizabeth reached for Pashanok and pointed toward the cliffs. Her heart stirred, her breath caught.

"Do you see how the light is falling?"

He glanced once and turned away. "Shadows," he said. "Nothing more."

"No," she insisted gently. "Look again. Doesn't it seem like—the shape of a—giant?"

Then, over the hush between waves, came a sound— low and rhythmic, carried on the first breath of dawn,

**"Kehutamuwô wutahkomuk,
WuneeKeesoq wutôôk…"**

Pashanok froze. It was his own chant—but deeper, older—vast as the sea itself.

Elizabeth followed his gaze upward. Hidden within the cliffs of Aquinnah, the towering shadow of a giant man swayed with the wind and the tide, his great head bowed toward them. Moshup's voice rolled down like distant thunder, joining Pashanok's in the final lines:

"Neesqutôtam nashpe papôut…"

As their voices merged, the sky itself seemed to lean in—the rising sun painted the eastern horizon in molten gold, while the great pale moon sunk toward the western sea, its light still silvering the foam.

Then as if by a miracle—they saw Môsi—running down the beach to them, arms in the air, dancing and spinning with joy!

"Mom! Dad! Look who it is!" She cried.
"He saved us!—He saved ME!"

Pashanok turned back and laughed with tears in his eyes, shaking his head, 'Moshup!"
Then—as if in answer—a wave unlike the others lifted their battered boat and carried it gently onto the sand. The sea settled. The shadow upon the cliffs thinned and stretched, becoming stone and wind once more.

High on the cliffs above stood the **Sachem Nokamoset.** Tobiasquash, Edgar and the Aquinnah elders gathered with other members of the tribe.

"The spirit who guards the deep has spoken to Môsi," Nokamoset offered, his voice low. "He has not done so to our people in many lifetimes."

An elder nodded. "Then it is true—the child carries both bloods, yet walks with Noepe's heart beneath her feet. As Moshup remembers her, he remembers us."

Below them, the beach was littered with flotsam and jetsam from the wreck. Broken masts and tattered sails still broke the water's surface along Devil's Bridge. Some of the Wampanoag searched for survivors, while others had already begun the work of salvage.

Nokamoset turned to them all.

"The cliffs of Aquinnah know Moshup's hand once again," he said. "The waters his breath. May the heart of Noepe's people always remain with their keeper."

— *Chapter 18* —

The morning after the storm, the sea breathed slow and heavy, each wave dragging its weight along the sand as though the ocean itself were weary. The first light of day spread like pale fire across the horizon, and the air carried the sharp scent of kelp and splintered pine.

Word of the wreck had traveled through the night on a single, tired horse, carrying Edgar and Tobiasquash from farm to farm along the south road with Argon trotting behind. By mid-afternoon, Chilmark families and Wampanoag from the nearby **wutahkomuk** had begun making their way down toward the shore. Among them were Reverend Mayhew and Wampanuit, each drawn by the same urgent news: Beth and Martha had been aboard the *Deliverance*.

People moved along the tide line—villagers in salt-stained coats and aprons, Wampanoag men and women in weather-darkened tunics. They kept to their own clusters at first, but all had come for the same reason. The wreck had left gifts in the surf, and at least a few survivors.

A crate of onions rolled in the shallows, its lid broken away. Two boys splashed after it, laughing. A young Wampanoag woman hauled a sodden coil of rope to the dry sand, shaking her head at its weight. Farther down the beach, a fisherman pried loose the lid of a barrel, grinning at the smell of salted fish inside. Every so often, a small cheer went up when something worth the struggle was found.

Then came a shout from two fishermen near the rocks. They dragged a man from the water, his hair plastered white with salt, eyes wild in terror. He clutched a broken oar like a weapon.

"A giant!" he gasped—staggering against the men's hold. "A giant rose from the deep! Took the ship in his hands! I saw it—I swear it on my soul!"

Some scoffed, calling him drunk or crazed, but others went quiet, stealing glances toward the Wampanoag who worked farther down the beach. The old stories of Moshup needed no reminding.

Martha moved along the shore with Argon at her side, his fur still stiff from salt. She was pale from exhaustion but walked steady, scanning the debris for anything of use. People turned to watch her pass, no longer with studied concern, but with the wary respect given to someone who had survived a thing others could only imagine. She stopped to help a villager she barely knew lift a half-waterlogged cask. He muttered his thanks, and before long others stepped forward to lend their strength.

Then Beth appeared with Pashanok at her side, both damp and weather-worn, yet unmistakably alive. The sight froze Reverend Mayhew in mid-step.

"Elizabeth—" he breathed, as though naming a ghost. His face broke into a smile of stunned relief. "By heaven, I thought you—" He stopped himself, glancing around at the crowd. "I was too late. I meant to see you freed by law, but the sea has spared me the trouble."

Beth gave him a faint smile, her voice even. "Much more than that, Reverend. Moshup was our savior. You'll have to thank him, not the sea."

Pashanok stood a pace behind her, his gaze calm and watchful. Wampanuit came forward, clasping his nephew's shoulder. Mayhew's gaze shifted to him, and in that moment the four of them—Elizabeth, Pashanok, Wampanuit, and Mayhew—stood as living symbols of the island's two peoples.

"It is a hard thing to lose so much to the sea," Mayhew said at last.

"And a good thing to take back what the sea gives," Wampanuit replied.

They spoke so all could hear, agreeing that the salvage would be shared according to need—for both peoples are of this island, and the island feeds us all. Their words carried in the salt air, and something in the crowd eased, like a knot slowly working loose.

Still, not every knot came free. Two women in dark cloaks—faceless critics like the graveyard gossips—stood apart, muttering to each other. Their eyes followed Beth with the same practiced suspicion as all who are like them, whispering of witchcraft and ruin. They made no move to help with the salvage.

Edgar worked nearby with Tobiasquash, hauling a heavy chest that leaked seawater with each step. His shoulders ached from the previous night's ride, but he said nothing. Tobiasquash grinned at him over the load.

"Worth the bruises?" he asked.

Edgar huffed a laugh. "Worth every one."

When the chest was stowed, Tobiasquash led Edgar over to a small group of tribal boys about his age. Introductions were awkward at first—curt nods, quick glances—but the boys eventually began showing Edgar the more unusual finds from the wreck: a carved ivory comb, a length of copper chain, a polished ship's compass.

A little farther down the beach, Wampanoag girls who had once jeered at Martha in the past, watched her from the edge of their mothers' work. They said nothing now, their faces solemn, respectful—but not yet friendly.

The sun began its descent, throwing gold across the water. The beach became a hive of motion—tribal and village hands alike hauling barrels, timbers, and sailcloth to higher ground. The sharp lines that had long divided them were blurred now, blurred by shared labor, shared salt spray, and the sight of the same storm-blackened horizon.

By late afternoon the beach was stripped of what could be saved and the rest surrendered back to the tide. Reverend Mayhew stood with Wampanuit at the head of the path, salt whitening their boots, and spoke low, so all could hear without shouting.

Wampanuit said with a sweeping gesture to the crowd. "Tonight—our drum will sound in honor to the Great Spirit."

"Let our bell ring true," Mayhew inclined his head towards parishioners nearby, "How the good Lord has blessed us from the bounty of the sea, and for the hands that gathered it together."

Before they parted, Reverend Mayhew and Wampanuit exchanged a final nod, the kind that no longer needs formality. Martha stood in the surf, Argon at her side, watching one group turn toward the Wampanoag village above, and the other toward the middle road.

Word ran ahead of them like a good wind. Barrels rolled inland on handcarts, nets slung over shoulders, children racing, Argon bounding between clusters as if to herd them all into one people. Martha walked beside Elizabeth and Pashanok, the three of them passing from cliffs to lane to village road, the last light gilding their faces. When they reached Chilmark green, someone struck the meetinghouse bell, and from the Aquinnah **wutahkomuk** beyond, an answering drum began to speak.

Martha saw the same determination in every back and felt the truth of it settle deep in her chest. The new music expressed a harmony no one had known before, resonating deep from the spirit within all people.

This, she thought, is how it should be. Somewhere beyond the fields and woodlands, her vineyard awaited, and she felt it, too, had weathered the storm.

— *Chapter 19* —

The air was thick with the golden hush of early autumn. Bees hovered lazily over the last wildflowers, and the sun cast long slanting rays across the island's ridges and hollows. The scent of wood smoke mingled with crushed grapes and drying seaweed, an old familiar perfume that signaled the start of the Harvest Festival.

For seven days, the Wampanoag gathered at the cliffs of Aquinnah—men, women, children, elders—dressed in their finest. Deerskin tunics dyed with berry and bark, woven sashes, bead-work, feathers, and painted faces gleamed in the flickering firelight of early evening. Each family brought their best: ears of corn stacked like pyramids, gourds painted with swirling fish and waterfowl, baskets heavy with clams, quahogs, roots, and blueberries. Even the animals seemed caught up in the spirit of celebration, trotting along behind their owners adorned with garlands of vine and shell.

From the moment she arrived, Martha felt something shift. It was not merely joy or ceremony—it was belonging. For the first time, she walked among the people of her father's blood as one of their own. She wore a stitched tunic dyed in the juice of her vineyard grapes—a deep purpling hue that stained her palms but brought her pride. Around her waist, a belt of braided sea grass. In her hands, a clay jug of the island's first grape drink — tangy and wild, barely fermented, and more beloved as much for its taste and the promise it held.

Children scampered past her barefoot, their laughter carrying through the pine trees. Tobiasquash came loping up, his arms painted in blue swirls and his chest smeared with ash like a bear. "They said I was too old to join the children's race," he panted. "So I started a man's race. First prize is three dried eels and Beth's purple wool. Second prize is my leftover eels."

Martha laughed. "Who's judging?"

"**Wussoquat**, obviously. Which means I'll win."

"Cheater."

"Who, me?" he said, grinning.

The festival was more than contests—though there were many. Archery and spear throws, wrestling matches, and rope climbing. Songs and drumming echoed through the woods and over the cliffs. Martha spotted nearly every child she had met that summer—even the shy boy who once refused to speak to her now presented her with a fistful of beach plums. She took them with a nod and whispered something in Wampanoag, which made him beam with pride.

Beth stood beneath a birch tree beside Pashanok and Nunaquas, laughing gently with her and sorting folded cloth into neat piles. Her purple-dyed wool, sun-faded into lavender and indigo, shimmered in the light. It was said to hold the color of the sea at dusk, and women from every tribal village came to run their fingers along the fabric. Beth had worried she wouldn't be accepted, but here, now, she belonged. The elder women had even braided her white hair with dyed strips of wool and placed a carved whale's tooth in the center like a brooch.

"She's smiling more," Pashanok said, appearing beside Martha. He carried a carved staff adorned with feathers and shells, and his quiet strength seemed more radiant now—as if the island itself had lent him its voice. "Even when she thinks no one sees."

Martha looked toward the fire where her mother sat and nodded. "That's how I know it's real."

By the third night, the sky flared with orange and magenta as the sun sank toward the ocean. A hush fell across the meadow as Nokamoset rose and walked quietly into the circle. The sachem stood tall in his years, his face deeply lined, his shoulders wrapped in a mantle of heron feathers. Children gathered close. Even the youngest ones stopped their chattering.

"WuneeKeesoq, Noepe **ohkeak**," he began—Good spirit, people of Noepe. He let the greeting carry over the gathered crowd before his voice deepened.

"From the stone, the tide, and the wind, we learn what endures," Nokamoset said, his voice like river gravel and cedar smoke. "The stories of Noepe are held within our spirit, and today we open our hearts to another."

He turned, slowly, until his gaze found Martha, "Môsi—the child delivered by Moshup, the daughter of two peoples, who keeps Noepe whole. We honor her for who she is—the root that joins our blood to the new clans of Noepe. She carries the old names and the new—an honest heart and a healing touch. She reminds us of who we are, and who we may yet become."

A murmured chant began—soft at first, like wind through reeds — then building, rhythmic, pulsing with drumbeat and voice. The children began to dance around her, holding hands while singing with joy—

Moshup kôhtakut!
Peequtamun nôeese!
Nôeesak wut Môsi Moshupash!

Moshup has returned!
Look upon our hearts!
Our hearts with Martha and Moshup!

Martha stepped forward, unsure, her heart pounding like thunder against bone. Someone placed a woven crown of shells and feathers on her head. Another draped her with a cloak stitched with grape leaves. She looked over and caught Elizabeth's eye. Her mother was smiling through tears. As the song drew to a close, the entire festival quietly turned their attention to the final moments of the day. With a brilliant green flash, the sun dipped below the horizon followed by their spontaneous cheer.

Later that night, the tribe lit a great fire atop the cliffs, visible to the ships miles at sea. Songs carried across the waves like birds on the wing. Pashanok played a reed flute. Beth's dyed wool fluttered from sticks like banners. And Martha, sitting cross-legged with her cousins, turned her face up to the stars and whispered the names of those who could not be with them — Caroline and others lost to storm and sickness — all remembered in the hush of flame and wind.

The moon rose as if casting a spell across Noepe, full and silver, and the sea glistened like glass all around.

As the fire crackled low and embers danced into the night, Nokamoset with Wampanuit and other tribal elders climbed to the edge of the cliff. Their silhouettes stood dark against the sky.

Nokamoset raised his staff high and spoke only once more:

Moshup watches the Wampanoag
in spirit and in love
when Noepe remembers itself
sons and daughters
Moshup returns

The Ancient One
delivered his daughter-spirit
from the waters
a living reminder
Moshup is always near

High atop the cliffs, the shadow of a great figure stood watch—or perhaps it was only the moon in the mist. But in that moment, the people believed.

And through believing, their hope was united.

Martha's story had just begun . . .

—Epilogue—

The vineyard lay quiet under the late-summer sun, its rows heavy with deep purple clusters. A warm wind drifted in from the sea, carrying the briny scent of the tide. Elizabeth—no longer hiding behind the name Beth—sat on the low stone wall, journal resting in her lap. The leather cover was worn smooth, the pages soft with years of turning.

It had been many seasons since she had opened it to write, yet now her hand seemed almost eager. She dipped her pen, paused, and let her eyes rest on the girl in the distance.

Martha moved between the vines with her hair loose and glinting in the light, speaking softly to each plant as if coaxing secrets from old friends. Argon trotted at her side, pausing now and then to nose the baskets brimming with grapes.

Elizabeth began to write, the words forming without hesitation:

There is a wildness to her still, as there always was—but it is no longer the wildness of the untamed. It is the wildness of the free. Martha belongs to the island as much as the sea belongs to the shore. The storms have not broken her. They have only deepened her roots.

Her pen slowed. She thought of the girl's first steps among these vines, of all the seasons of growth and change, and of the truth that had finally come to light between them.

In the meadow beyond, Tobiasquash and Edgar rode up on bare-backed horses, dismounting to help gather the harvest. Their laughter mixed with Martha's voice, and Elizabeth realized she was smiling.

She wrote one final line, her hand steady:

No matter what the years bring, she will keep this place alive—and it will keep her.

Elizabeth closed the book with quiet finality and placed it on the wall beside her. The breeze lifted a loose strand of her white hair, and she looked toward the sea.

Beyond the stone wall, Martha's voice carried on the wind, speaking to the vines in the old tongue, claiming the land as her own.

Noepe—the island the English would soon call Martha's Vineyard.

— Wampanoag Glossary —

This glossary is divided into three sections: Character Names - Places and Words - Chants.

It's purpose is to honor and reflect the Wôpanâak (Wampanoag) language and its cultural significance within the story. Some entries are based on historically documented words and their reconstructed pronunciations; others are respectfully hybridized or interpretive, constructed from known linguistic roots, context, and oral tradition to support fictional use in Martha: The Vineyard Legend.

Where possible, definitions aim to preserve poetic or metaphorical meaning in addition to literal translation. Every effort has been made to ensure accuracy and cultural sensitivity, while also supporting the immersive experience of readers unfamiliar with the language. We encourage further learning and engagement through recognized resources such as the Wôpanâak Language Reclamation Project (WLRP)

– Wampanoag Glossary –
Character Names

This section includes constructed and traditional Wampanoag names used for characters in Martha – The Vineyard Legend. Each entry includes pronunciation and meaning, with notes on etymology and interpretive choices. - See Footnote below.

Keesoq (KEE-sook) – Great Spirit, Sky Being, Creator – A powerful spiritual name evoking the supreme sky deity or guiding force. Closely associated with light, the heavens, and divine watchfulness.

Maskotae (MASS-ko-tay) – A Wampanoag male name, derived from Algonquian maskotee meaning "prairie, meadow, or open land." Connotes one connected to wide, open spaces and the hunt.

Mattaniqua (mat-TAH-nee-kwah) – "She who remembers" or "mother spirit" – A constructed feminine name blending native elements to suggest ancestral memory, nurturing wisdom, and spiritual femininity.

Moshup (MOH-shup) – Giant of Wampanoag legend who shaped the land – A central figure in tribal lore, credited with forming geographical features such as the **Aquinnah** cliffs. Seen as both protector and force of nature.

Môsi (MOH-see) – Beloved daughter of two peoples

Nokamoset (noh-KAH-moh-set) – "Grandfather-like one" or "wise elder" – A reverent term used for a tribal elder, often a sachem or wisdom figure. Combines the root for grandparent (*nókamos*) with a masculine or honorific suffix.

Nunaquas (NOO-nah-kwahs) – "Soft wind" or "quiet river woman" – A gentle and graceful feminine name constructed from roots meaning water or breath. Conveys calm resilience and maternal dignity.

Pashanok (PAH-sha-nock) – "He who watches" or "the silent one who sees" – A constructed masculine name evoking perceptiveness and vigilance. Inspired by *pashôet* (he sees).

Sôpan (SOH-pahn) – – She goes forth or moves ahead. A girl's name evoking motion, independence, or new beginnings.

Tawasquat (tah-WAHS-kwat) – "Distant thunder" or "echoing strength" – A poetic name suggesting powerful presence and internal force. Inspired by roots implying sound, storm, or rumble.

Tawôtam (tah-WOH-tahm) – "Strong of body" or "one who is vigorous"

Tobiasquash (toh-BYE-ah-squash) – "Young mischief" or "he who breaks trail with laughter" – A hybrid of colonial and tribal naming. 'Tobias' reflects biblical influence, while '-quash' evokes a playful, trail-blazing spirit.

Wampanuit (WAHM-pah-noo-it) – "Eastern seer" or "he speaks the dawn"; a name for a medicine man or spiritual guide.

Wunnêgin (wuh-NAY-gin) – Peace; harmony; goodness. A girl's name meaning "she brings peace."

Wussoquat (WUSS-oh-kwat) – "Dark breeze" or "whispering branch"; name with shadowy or ambiguous connotations — secretive or quietly opposing.

Wuttahmin (WUH-tah-min) – A Wampanoag male name, derived from the Algonquian root wutahmin meaning "grape" or "fruit of the vine." Symbolic of abundance and nourishment, fitting for a fisher and provider.

– Wampanoag Glossary –

Places and Words

This section includes Wampanoag and reconstructed Wôpanâak terms used in the story *Martha – The Vineyard Legend*. Entries include place names, vocabulary, and cultural terms. Each is presented with pronunciation and meaning, and where applicable, interpretive notes.

ahtuck (AH-tuck) – Deer

ahtuck nôp (AH-tuhk nohp) – Deerskin – Literally 'deer skin/hide'; 'nôp' means skin or hide

Aquinnah (ah-KWIN-nah) – "Land under the hill" or "low land"; modern name for the westernmost town on Martha's Vineyard, historically home to the Wampanoag people

Cheppiaquidne (chep-pee-AH-kwid-nuh) — Wampanoag: "separated island."Refers to the eastern island now called Chappaquiddick, connected to Noepe (Martha's Vineyard) by a narrow strip of sand.

cheecheemoo (chee-CHEE-moo) – – Rabid/mad dog; a term used for a frenzied or cursed animal, metaphorically for danger or madness

chôkannês (choh-KAHN-ness) – – Soldier; warrior in arms — A person trained or assigned to fight, especially in structured or colonial military terms

eskwete'wi (ess-kweh-TAY-wee) – It is dusk; the time when light fades, symbolic of transition

Katama (kah-TAH-mah) – "Crab-fishing place"; a region of Martha's Vineyard traditionally used by the Wampanoag for shellfishing and seasonal habitation

keesoqâw (KEE-soh-kaw) – He/she is a spirit person

kuhkum (KOO-koom) – Grandmother; a term of familial respect and elder affection

maneechuwô (mah-NEE-choo-woh) – Spirit-being or mystical figure; sometimes used to refer to a deity or shapeshifter in Wampanoag lore

Mashpee (MASH-pee) – "Great water" or "place near the water"; a historic Wampanoag community and town on Cape Cod

maskutash (muhs-KOO-tash) – Poultice or healing plant mixture

moashoon (moh-AH-shoon) – Canoe

mukquosh (muhk-KWOH-sh) – Owl

mushum (MOO-shoom) – Grandfather; a term of reverence for a male elder

m'suhtam (m-SOO-tum) – He/she understands

namohs (NAH-moss) – Fish

nanapashômut (nah-nah-pah-SHOW-moot) – One who comes from far away

nanapashômutash (nah-nah-pah-SHOW-moo-tash) – Those who come from far away

Narragansett (nair-uh-GAN-sit) – A neighboring Algonquian-speaking tribe from what is now Rhode Island

netahtunuw (neh-TAH-too-noo) - cousin

Noepe (NOH-eh-peh) – "Land amid the waters"; the Wampanoag name for Martha's Vineyard

nôtam (NOH-tahm) – He/she listens

nôônâmês (noh-oh-NAH-mess) – Rat or mouse; small gnawing rodent

nuppanashômut (noo-PAH-nah-show-moot) – One who finds the way / discovers a path

nuxkáawees (nuhx-KAH-wees) – Sister

ohkeak (OH-kee-ahk) – Land / earth; pluralized as "lands" or "people of the land." Used in *Noepe ohkeak*

ohkeema (oh-KEE-mah) – Chief; leader or one who governs a tribal group

payaus (PAI-yahs) – He/she runs

pôhkomash (POH-ko-mash) – goat; formed from *pôhkom* (horned one) and *ash* (a suffix for animals), creating a Wampanoag term for a non-native animal.

pôhtam (POH-tahm) - Whale

pohtap (POH-tahp) – Fire

ponaw (POH-nahw) – He/she helps

powwaw (POW-waw) – Spiritual leader or shaman; one who intercedes between the natural and spirit worlds

pâhqashawut (PAH-qah-shah-wut) – She who stands for the people

pâwâhsuw (PAH-wah-soo) – whippoorwill; a night bird whose cry is linked to omens, messages, and spirit signs.

sôtyum (SOH-tee-um) – fool; used playfully as an insult, similar in tone to "silly" or "foolish."

squaëses (SKWAH-es-sis) – young girl / female child.

Tequenoman (teh-KEH-noh-mahn) – Island beyond the known waters – A poetic or archaic Wôpanâak name referring to what is now called Nomans Land

Wampanoag (WAHM-puh-nog) – "People of the First Light"; the tribal nation of southeastern Massachusetts

wampompeag (WAHM-pom-pag) – Wampum; beads made from the purple and white shells of the **popôq** (quahog). Worn as ornament, recorded as memory, and used in diplomacy, ceremony, and trade.

weti (WEH-tee) – locative form meaning in or at the wetu.

wetu (WEH-too) – Wampanoag dwelling or house, typically made of bark or mats over a wooden frame

wopanaakok (WOH-puh-nah-kok) – The Wampanoag people (plural)

wuneeKeesoq (woo-NEE-kee-suk) – Good day; a greeting.

wunnêgin (wuh-NAY-gin) – Beautiful – A term meaning "beautiful" or "pleasant" in appearance

wuskëtom (wuss-KEH-tum) – Pine tree or pine wood – Refers to the pine tree itself or the wood derived from it

wuskóonk (WUSS-konk) – hair; head hair – Refers broadly to the hair on one's head, reconstructed from Wôpanâak sources.

wusqôhs (WOOS-kohs) – Rabbit

wutahkomuk (woo-TAH-koh-muck) – dwelling place; a village or settlement composed of multiple **weti** (dwellings). In Wampanoag usage, this refers to a community site where families live and work, rather than a colonial "town" with formal government.

wuttawâm (wuh-tuh-WAHM) – Truth

— Wampanoag Glossary —

Chants

Children's Chant to Moshup
(Chapter 7)

Kishkuwôk nashau, Moshup!
(KISH-koo-wock NAH-shah, MOE-shup)

Peequtamun-nôeese!
(pee-koo-TAH-mun nuh-WEE-suh)

Translation / Meaning:
"West wind, Moshup — look upon our hearts!"
A chant sung by children in playful devotion, connecting
the west wind with Moshup's protection and guidance.

Sea & Sky Chant
(Chapter 15)

Kehutamuwô wutahkomuk,
(keh-HOO-tah-moo-woh woo-TAH-ko-muk)

Nôpaheesu nashpe kesuq,
(noh-pah-HAY-soo NASH-peh KAY-sooq)

Nôpaheesu nashpe tôk,
(noh-pah-HAY-soo NASH-peh TOOK)

Kehutamuwô kehkitôk,
(keh-HOO-tah-moo-woh keh-kee-TOOK)

Neesqutôtam nashpe papôut.
(NEE-skwoo-toh-tahm NASH-peh pah-POH-wut)

Translation / Meaning:

Hear me, great ocean,
Bright sun in the sky,
I rise from the deep,
Hear me, great wind,
Stand with me in the storm.

A ceremonial chant — Pashanok calls upon while preparing to intercept Morgrave's ship. It invokes the elemental spirits of sea, sun, and wind for strength.

Harvest Festival Chant
(Chapter 19)

Moshup kôhtakut!
(MOE-shup KOH-tah-kut)

Peequtamun nôeese!
(pee-koo-TAH-mun nuh-WEE-suh)

Nôeesak wut Môsi Moshupash!
(NUH-wee-sahk wut MOE-see MOE-shup-ash)

Translation / Meaning:

Moshup has returned!
Look upon our hearts!
Our hearts with Martha and Moshup!

Sung during the Harvest Festival to honor Martha (Môsi)
as a child of both peoples and Moshup's symbolic
daughter. It unites the community in gratitude and
recognition of her role.

Closing Poem of Nokamoset
(Chapter 19)

Wôpanâak
(reconstructed form**)**

Moshup wôkwsuwôk Wampanoag
(MOE-shup WOHK-soo-wok WAHM-pa-nog)

nashpe wôntun nashpe wuneetôonk
(NAH-shpe WOHN-tun NAH-shpe woo-NEE-tunk)

**Tahshe Noepe wuneekeesuwôk ohkeak —
mushqush nash netompash**
(TAH-shay NO-ee-pee woo-nee-KEE-soo-wok OHK-ee-ak
— MOOSH-koosh NAH-sh net-OM-pash)

Moshup pishqayut
(MOE-shup PISH-kai-yut)

Kehteanit
(keh-TEE-ah-nit)

wutôpuhsuwôk nôkushun
(woo-TOH-puh-soo-wok NOH-koo-shun)

nashpe nippe
(NAH-shpe NIP-pay)

wôpanâak nôkushun
(woh-pah-NAH-ak NOH-koo-shun)

Moshup anqutôonk
(MOE-shup AHN-koo-toonk)

Translation / Meaning:

Moshup watches the Wampanoag
in spirit and in love
When Noepe remembers itself — sons and daughters
Moshup returns
The Ancient One
delivered his daughter-spirit
from the waters
a living reminder
Moshup is always near

A prayerful chant —This final chant reminds the people
that Moshup's presence is not bound by time or distance.
Though hidden from ordinary sight, his spirit watches
over the Wampanoag in love, guiding them as a parent
watches over children. The island of Noepe itself carries
memory, and when its sons and daughters honor that
memory, Moshup will return — not as a figure of the
past, but as a living force in the present. The chant recalls
the Ancient One's gift: the daughter-spirit brought safely
from the waters, a reminder that Moshup is always near,
ready to protect and renew his people whenever they call
upon him.

Learning Wampanoag

The Wôpanâak (Wampanoag) language carries a worldview where land, people, and spirit are inseparable. Words are not just labels but relationships, each one alive with memory. This story uses Wampanoag terms sparingly, but enough to invite readers into the rhythm of the language.

Here is a simple example:

Kuhkeesuq wôpanêak kusêhtuqutahsh tápuonk. Ohke wusôhsun wutunâhtuq.

"The girl walks quietly between the trees. The land remembers her."

This sentence shows how Wampanoag thought emphasizes connection. The girl is not just moving through a forest — the land itself is aware of her presence, remembering her as part of it.

Wampanoag language often joins the speaker to the world around them. It reminds us that people, land, and history are bound together, and that memory lives in place as much as in story. We must also remember how people lived much closer to the natural world than we do today. In the 1600s, life was more like camping all the time — no light switches to flip, no cars to drive, no grocery stores to visit. Every meal depended on what they could grow in their gardens, and meat came from their own animals or from the butcher in town. Survival meant paying attention to the land, because it provided everything.

Sources & Language Acknowledgment

The Wôpanâak words and meanings included in this glossary draw primarily from the following sources:

Wôpanâak Language Reclamation Project (WLRP) – www.wlrp.org

Glosbe Wampanoag Dictionary – https://glosbe.com/

Native Languages of the Americas – www.native-languages.org

Historical records from colonial-era translations, such as John Eliot's Wampanoag Bible (1663) and related Algonquian dictionaries Supplemental guidance from related Algonquian dialects when Wampanoag equivalents are unknown or extinct.

Some words in this glossary are interpretive reconstructions, crafted for poetic clarity or narrative function while remaining rooted in Wôpanâak structure or meaning. All usage is done with respect and admiration for the language and its people.

— Author's Note —

When I first traveled to Martha's Vineyard as a boy, I wondered: Who is Martha? And, Where are all the grapes? Eventually, I moved to the island and lived in Edgartown during my twenties and thirties. Still, many visitors were still asking the same questions.

This novel is my answer — not in the form of a historical record, but as a legend. It imagines how the name, the place, and the people might have come together in Martha's story. While woven with historical threads, it is not a documentary account. Any fictionalizations are made with reverence for the people of Noepe and the enduring Wampanoag legacy.

To the Wampanoag people, whose resilience and beauty have shaped the island for thousands of years — thank you for your presence, your language, and your stories. The zenith of your population was close to five thousand people in the 1600's, an incredible tribute to your culture and governing leadership. To the people of Martha's Vineyard past and present, thank you for holding space for mystery and meaning. And to the land itself — the cliffs, the wind, the waters, and the soil — you are the truest muse I've ever known.

— Maxwell Burnham

— Coming Soon —

Martha's story is only just beginning. While her adventures continue on Noepe, shadows gather beyond the island's shores. From the crowded docks of New Amsterdam to the hidden harbors of Great Harbor, children vanish — and so begins the tale of —

Runaway Orphan.

Martha —
The Vineyard Legend

Runaway Orphan

Maxwell Burnham

—*Prologue*—

The morning sun rose like a coin over New Amsterdam, gilding the docks and rooftops in sharp yellow. In the narrow shade between two fish stalls, a boy of fourteen stood recounting a harrowing tale to a small knot of children. He wore an embroidered vest too fine for his station, polished boots too stiff with salt, and a ring that slid freely over his knuckle as he gestured with flair.

"A giant savage, I tell you! Dark as night, bigger than the tallest mast," Skip whispered dramatically. "He stood on the red cliffs, roared like thunder, and drove the mighty ship straight into Devil's Bridge. Killed a dozen men just with his stare."

The children gasped—two boys of nine or ten, a brown-skinned girl clutching a satchel, and a lanky older youth with a shock of golden hair.

"You're lying," said the blond boy. "My uncle heard it was a storm."

"Storm and savage," Skip corrected. "Besides, ask any sailor what really sank the Deliverance. Go on, ask. They'll say it was me who saved Captain Blackburn—jumped from the wreck, swam three leagues in shark infested water, and dragged him to shore by his belt."

The brown-skinned girl frowned. "You swam with sharks?"

"Could've wrestled one, if I hadn't been so hungry,"

Skip replied. "But Captain Blackburn—he's generous, see. Took me in. Fed me. Gave me clothes like these." He tugged on his vest and turned so the brass buttons caught the light. "He's got a ship again now. Says he's lookin' for good hands. Maybe even a cabin girl."

The girl's eyes lit up.

"Come aboard, just for a look," Skip said smoothly. "There's stew today. New linens. Warm beds. You can even keep your satchel."

Hesitation flickered in a few eyes, but hunger and wonder outweighed it. Five children followed him through the alleys and up the gangplank of a weathered merchant vessel docked just past the customs building.

"Mind your step," Skip called back. "Captain likes tidy feet."

A tall sailor in a striped shirt guided them below deck. The passage narrowed and darkened. The door to the forward cabin swung open with a creak.

"In you go, little shipmates," the sailor said.

The children entered cautiously.

The door slammed shut.

A bolt scraped into place.

For a moment, silence. Then a boy's voice from the shadows:

"You'll want to sit against the hull. Not near the bucket."

The blond boy spun around. "Who said that?"

A figure stepped forward—older than the others, with dark skin and close-cropped hair. His shirt was torn, one eye swollen.

"Name's Dmitri," he said. "You're at the bottom now. But there's time to learn."

"To learn what?" asked the brown-skinned girl.

"Who not to cross. Who gets the scraps. Where to sleep without getting kicked. That kind of thing."

One of the new boys lunged for the door and pounded his fists. "Let us out!"

Dmitri didn't move. "They won't come. Not till we dock. Maybe not even then."

The air thickened with fear. A younger child began to cry softly. The brown-skinned girl hugged her satchel tighter.

Above deck, Skip sauntered along the rail, whistling. He found Captain Blackburn puffing on a clay pipe near the helm, scanning the horizon.

"Cargo's on board, sir," Skip said, hands in his pockets.

The captain didn't turn. "How many this time?"

"Four boys, one girl."

Blackburn blew a smoke ring. "Good. We'll put in at Great Harbor on Martha's Vineyard, then on to bonny London. Been too long dragging bilge rats around the Colonies. I miss civility."

"Good thing they fetch fine coinage, sir." Skip jangled his vest pocket and grinned. "Even if we lose a few along the way."

Martha —
The Vineyard Legend

Runaway Orphan

Be sure to read on in Martha's gripping legend saga as Skip returns to Martha's Vineyard, carrying forward his mentor's legacy of deception and cruelty. Martha will face not only the cunning of those who prey on the vulnerable, but also the rising tide of betrayal and power that threatens to consume her island.

The storm has passed —
but a darker tide is rising.

About the Author

Maxwell Burnham grew up surrounded by woods and open fields in the coastal town of Duxbury, where childhood afternoons often turned into adventures of imagination. Acting out frontier stories in the trees and meadows as a boy gave him a firsthand sense of how children of the 1600's might have seen the world—curious, resourceful, and alive with possibility.

Later, he lived in Edgartown on Martha's Vineyard, where the island's history, culture, and landscape left a lasting imprint. Those years helped inspire Martha — The Vineyard Legend, blending personal memory with the deeper heritage of Noepe and its people.

Today, Burnham writes stories that weave together history, myth, and imagination—tales that honor the past while inspiring readers of every age.